#21: Romance

July 2023

ROM - ROMANCE

EDITORIAL

EDITORS-IN-CHIEF: Mickey Collins & Robert Eversmann

MANAGING EDITORS: Michael Santiago & Z.B. Wagman

POETRY: Sarah Denison, Timothy Arliss OBrien, Jihye Shin &
        Nicholas Yandell

PROSE: Sarah Denison, Michael Santiago & Z.B. Wagman

ADDITIONAL COPYEDITING: Lorenzo Fusini & Heather Hambley

COVER: "Season For Love" by Joy Richu

CONTACT: editors@deepoverstock.com

On the Shelves

continued...

continued...

Letter from the Editors

Dearest Readers,

We love you. We want to take you on a date, woo you, bring you home to meet our parents and our cat. We'll cover you in kisses, or hold your hand, or just sit across the table from you with a knowing look in our eyes. We'll spend long days sitting in the same room reading to ourselves or each other in front of the lit fireplace, if that's what you want. And you've told us what you want and we're going to give you all that and more.

In the pages you hold near and dear to your heart we have tales of meet cutes, of awkward teenage loves, of crushes and lusts, of long-lasting relationships, relationships gone right and wrong, the love of another person, a physical thing, or idea. Treasure these stories and poems while they're here. Let them sit with you awhile and share their desires.

After you have been sufficiently romanced, prepare for something that will string you along and tie you up in complications. Our next issue *Knots* will be open for submissions until August 31st. Don't be afraid to be naughty.

With love, always,

Deep Overstock Editors

FINGERBANG!
By RJ Equality Ingram

Synopsis

A series of attempts made by a now defunct
Book club to break off an engagement
Before it happens what starts off as bad
Advice given at a New Years Eve party
Turns into a comedy of errors when an
Alcoholic poet recruits estranged frenemies
And former roommates alike while touring
A closing light exhibit at the local zoo
But who the hell would have expected a yes
To a proposal at the nail salon?! the last
Shot the poet has to end the engagement
Comes in the form of a sabotaged seance
But does RJ have the guts to tilt the spirit
Board's response to undo the mess he made?

Act I

How did you know? the architect asked
Midway through flute at the midnight party
Passing around dressings of gold leaves &
Honey the poet spoke about nail polish
Colors like *sleeping spoon* & *tambourine tan*
This is how I knew they were the one: Agony
Was all the time that we were not married
The only solution was a remedy by law
Or the gathering of dancers & bartenders
United under a buckeye tree to surrender
To no foreseeable limit the extent of tender
Reciprocated settings of simultaneous suns
My Evil Twin stepped out of balance played
Music from long drives into long headlights

Act II

The elephant's name was Bird of Paradise
Which meant you're never going to believe
Who is marrying   The poet & the dancer
The river townsfolk rumored on w/ stories
From grandfather walrus & uncle polo who
Also can't drink like their inner pirates surely
But *that* wasn't the end of it & the heavy bale
That held up the straw for the pack to eat
Mid afternoon flew away an hour early &
Where did he ask the proverbial question?
Don't tell me it was as bad as the salon?
That wasn't the point the point was eagles
Know how to sext too & immediately post
Coitus probably wasn't the classiest either

Act III

Digging in nail beds at the yuppie salon
Where rockabilly sober [or at least sober
In theory!] gentlethems sling acrylic Miro
Reproductions on thirsty himbos from
Down the block who know a thing or two
About the Russian Avant Garde & yes!
We have club cards but listen I know we
Think weddings are more than enjambment
Six nail techs file down at the same time
Listen to what the poet says not the alcoholic
The poet who pinches sleep from eyelashes
Fourteen years is a lot of work he says
We haven't felt it all at once though bc we
Share the rocks we carry from the river

Intermission

Brought to you by your friends at Fingerbang!
Your local beauty bar where martini & mani
Round up to a hundred real easily a really
Good reason to stay sober bc it's always
Been money for alcohol but now you can

Treat yo self! which sounds nuts bc when
Haven't you treated yourself? you're about
That got to get the fingers sticky while the
Honey's good but newsflash: swapping an
Addiction out for a reward gets old after
The seventh acrylic fill plus you're gonna
Need to do the dishes eventually or someone
Might notice that you actually don't enjoy
The way they scrape the back of your throat

Act IV

Back behind the scenes piles of books
Litter the production areas & one by one
The poet & the baker & the chemist &
The singer & the illustrator resurrect dead
Pages from Persephone's marble bedside
Fairy godparents to long neglected choruses
Of borrowed religions plus another 12 steps
All great surveyors of honest conversation
So the poet thinks he can outmaneuver
Every choice he's already made w/ regret
But not this time: RJ for once listen to yourself
No one blames you for trying to fix things
In ways only you could see as reasonable
Invite them over! bring out the spirit board!

Act V

Before my inevitable apology I need to say
My parents didn't lock me in a box but
Sometimes a real bad metaphor becomes
A real locked car on a late summer's day
And when I knocked the shot glass away
From my Evil Twin's hand I knew we had
Made the right choice & ended that agony
Fourteen years before but not before plays
Ended the same way the elephant reached
Up for the out of reach straw even though
She had no reason to reach in the first place
The poet folded the board it's a wash

The way he continues to compare wishes
Well how did *you* know? Always first things

Eye Contact
by Karen Sleeth

She looked up from her book, her eyes pulled like a magnet to the red-feathered black fedora.Grandpa had worn a dark gray one, much the same. She smiled and looked back to her story but she had lost her taste for its banality in contrast to the memory of Grandpa's dapper demeanor. Cherry blossom petals floated past her bench on hot-dog scented breezes, while she sought the fedora among a smattering of heads that circled the park at lunchtime. With mostly baseball caps and loose hair it wasn't difficult to locate the black domed hat. Its thin curved feather gave her tummy a delighted tickle and her mouth automatically curved upward as her gaze shifted below the brim to blue eyes. They were a crystalline azure against his tanned skin and her breath jammed as her smile became an *ooh*. And in silent reverence she stood as his eyes captured hers, and her *oooh* seized his.

Bicycle
by Paul Hostovsky

Now I would rather remember life than live it.
I would rather imagine life than live it.
I'd rather watch life going on from the sidelines
in a comfortable chair than stand in the midst of life
living it. And maybe that strikes you as sad
or perverse. And maybe I'm kind of a perv
because I'd rather watch some young people making love
than make love myself. And I would rather
read a poem about bicycles than ride a bicycle–I am done
riding bicycles. I am done making love. I am, sadly,
too old for that shit now. But I will never
be too old for the memory or the thought or the idea
of making love. Or the word *bicycle*. Which is
as good a word as any. And better than most. In fact,
I think *bicycle* will be my last word, my dying word–
not *I love you*, or *bless you*, or *God forgive me*,
but *bicycle*. And the people standing over me–
if there are any people standing over me at the last–
will look at each other and ask if they heard me right–
"Did he say *bicycle*?" "Yes, it sounded like *bicycle*"–
as I remember or imagine us riding our bicycles
in a summer rain, abandoning them on the edge of a wheat field,
taking off all our clothes–because it was raining
and we were soaked and hot and young–and running
naked through the field in the rain, and then, breathless,
sinking down in that field and making love. I don't
want to *be* in the field, in the rain, with the bugs and spiders
and rodents, the roots and stalks digging into my skin,
the itchy stems and leaves, a rat snake slithering past
and me freaking out and losing my erection–I just
want to remember or imagine two overturned bicycles
abandoned on the edge of a field, in which we were young
and soaked and happy and making love, kickstands
pointing randomly up toward heaven.

Sexting at Sixty
by Valerie Anne Burns

My cream-colored shrug so easily slipped off my shoulders and ran down my arms to the floor. This is not what I had envisioned as necessary to break the ice and the process of melting away fear and self-consciousness. He saw and felt no fear, only assured of his movements, which were seductive, and I wondered where my scars were because he did not see them. He didn't even see them under the blush colored and thin double strapped lace bra. My cheeks blushed to match the bra that fell to the floor near the shrug. My eyes glanced down at the fallen attire along with my fallen modesty.

* * *

There comes a time in a single woman's life when it is no longer wise to believe that a tailor-made Prince will knock gently at your door. Two decades past divorce and far too many start-ups that went south—far too many dating sites that proved to be more about scammers, a man holding a dead fish in a profile photo, or a profile photo resembling Charles Manson tends to wear a woman down.

A surprising day presented itself, one that was suited for an old-fashioned diary once written in as a blushing young woman. I was convinced the afternoon was guided by a Universal Power.

After my friend's late arrival from Los Angeles and indecisiveness, involving detours on where we wanted to land for our tete-a-tete in the perfect environment, we finally arrived at one of our favorite and sexiest spots in the Riviera hills of Santa Barbara.

We were told that a piatio table wasn't available, so we were directed to the bar. I couldn't help noticing people being seated at *our* special sofa two-top. The delay was a faux pas on the part of staff.

With hunger and impatience rising, we were finally seated. We took a big breath of serenity and indulged in flutes of sparkling rosé. While chatting with my friend who paused to respond to a sext message from her Latin paramour with a big smile on her face, I noticed a feeling of envy surge through me. We moved in the direction of speaking about the challenges of romance as we sunk down in the sofa for further comfort. I told my friend how I'd come to a place of realization by saying, "I just may be single for the rest of my days, especially since it had been an incessant period I'd been romantically connected to a man."

I stumbled and shamefully blurted out my sentiments on the horror of going through years of a breast cancer ordeal. Followed by stating, "If a miracle would appear and bless me with a desirable man, it would take an indeterminable amount of time to trust anyone after going through so much trauma." I went further and said, "The type of man I'd be interested in close to my age wants a woman 10-20 years younger and that is a damn fact." I had witnessed it repeatedly on the deeply discouraging internet dating sites. My friend took it all in and said, "You're still beautiful and there is always hope." I smiled at her in gratitude as my eyes closed and inhaled the eucalyptus scent to push away the feeling of hopelessness I went to bed with every night.

I thought that I was past my torrid affairs, which I'd clung to as I grew older. I drifted from these inner thoughts back to the splendid view and light-hearted girl talk when a tall, dark, and arresting gentleman suddenly appeared to offer his apologies for the major employee mishap. It is a 5-Star property, and this was the man acting as private consultant to work out the troubling kinks to ensure they remain 5-star. After finally obtaining our prized seat on a sofa with luxe pillows, sipping our glass of sparkling rose, eating California cuisine, and a good hour of staring past the eucalyptus grove to the deep blue sea while conversing like teenagers, we didn't care much. This gentleman, nevertheless, comped us a second sparkling rosé at $32 a glass.

I got up to make my way to the restroom and carefully walked from the terrace to the lobby, where said gentleman, with an unusual name I never quite caught, passed me coming the other direction. Catching his eye, something electrical immediately ran right through me and nearly stopped me from moving forward. Was it a ghost of a past life? A sexual spark hit me… hard.

I was torn between backing away and pushing toward him. He was immediately turned on. Do I still have that effect? He's so much younger than me and I found myself being drawn back to days when my sexual prowess was consistent. So much has passed in the choppy currents of life since then. He grabbed my face, and I was brought back to the moment in a jolt of sensual power with his purposeful kiss telling me exactly what path this rendezvous would go down.

My spunky friend and I dragged ourselves from the elegant terrace enjoying the deep golden red of sunset lighting the trees and table with a magic-hour glow. I looked for the gentleman that had kindly comped our drinks to thank him, but he disappeared, as did thoughts of attraction, which were more than likely a result of pale pink bubbles in a flute. I laid in bed thinking how silly to be convinced of a super-energy with someone at least a decade younger. Regardless, a well-deserved polite thank you to the man whose energy shot through my body as if the spirit of a significant past lover from another century seemed right.

"Wait, wait, I'm not ready… I feel embarrassed."

A barely whispered, "Why?"

I no longer knew.

I figured I would reach the hostess and ask her to pass along a thank you when I phoned the next day, but I didn't expect her to say, "He's standing right here." I simply wanted to thank him for coming to the aid of two women. I heard an enthusiastic baritone voice on the other end of the phone. He knew who I was and after a polite and brief conversation he said, "Let's meet for a drink downtown." I was convinced that it was a matter of a friendly gesture toward a local, and he would welcome a change of scenery on an evening off.

Sitting in a wicker chair on the patio of a wine bar, I met the gentleman originally from a region that straddles both Europe and Asia and a US citizen for decades with a permanent residence a couple states away. He was residing and working in town at a piece of heaven in the hills—a temporary position. Had there not been an unexplained staff screw-up, we would have never crossed paths.

I had a top shelf shot of Tequila. I was told by a healer that it is pure and doesn't give you a hangover. It wasn't a romantic date. But it was a welcomed diversion to meet-up with someone I met organically as opposed to the dreadful internet dating. He was the perfect age of fifty. Conversation was easy and flowed without a hint of strain. Since it couldn't be a date, especially with the age gap, I was at ease to be candid. He wanted to know about me, my book, my background. His background was something hard to imagine—a land of ancient history, and poetry.

When I stepped away, he ordered me another shot of tequila. My balance was off from both alcohol *and* him. I was careful to not finish the second shot. I was already tipsy, and keenly aware of how long it had been since I'd been in the company of a striking man whose tempting masculinity excited me, which led me to chatting up a storm. He didn't mind.

I was easily spilling personal information by a confidence-induced shot of tequila since he was simply someone interesting, cultured, well-traveled and educated (possessing four fluent languages) to talk to, which is a rarity in this small resort town. He continued to probe me about my book and what inspired me to write a memoir. I revealed I'm a breast cancer survivor, which is not something I would be inclined to reveal on a first date. The telling of a convoluted breast cancer ordeal is only a small part of my book, but it has been a big part of my life the last several years.

He divulged being divorced with three young kids. I switched the discussion back to his culture and all the places he'd traveled to and lived—sitting with a man enjoying verbal stimulation was a wonderful departure from daily routine. I told him about my upcoming travels to Italy. It had been a while since I was lifted to a feeling of pleasure by being fully engaged in an exchange with a man where I could share both joys and pains.

A sip of a second shot of tequila prickled down to my toes, and I quickly turned shy and nervous around his robust maleness oozing from every pore. I felt out-of-control. This is what Tinder dates must lead to and then women get in trouble. I was in trouble. I'd drifted so far out to sea in my isolation that it was nothing like getting back on a bike again. Was he pulling me into his shore?

My jeans were on the floor. My hands over my stomach that's no longer completely flat. I was grateful for not wearing one of my surgical bras, which I often do since it's easy and not confining. As I was standing there, no longer 50 years old and unsure of which part of my body to hide, he said, "You have a beautiful body." He moved his hands down to my navel and then to my back and hips where I heard a near inaudible groan.

Suddenly, as I was scanned up and down from long legs, stretched out in front of me, with a pair of stylish coco colored suede sandals, to the nice top and makeup well-applied to my pink flushed face, I heard a compliment. Wait, what? "You look really nice; you have great style." Did I detect a hint of lust in his compliment? Yes, I'm not that off in my intuition and it was the look in his nearly black eyes that looked like discs sending a shivered thrill to every cell. I became too aware of myself with heat rising to my head. If it were a date, it'd take more occasions of getting together before I could open myself to sex after all the assault to my body—losing my breasts, losing the erotic feeling from cutting all the nerves… no longer feeling like myself. The energy I felt since we first made eye contact was undoubtedly exhilarating but also unnerving.

I needed to go and knew to get home before dark. We'd been together more than two hours on a warm August evening. We took a brief stroll. He wanted to drive me home but how would I get my car the next day? He insisted on at least follow-ing me to be assured of my safety.

I said, "It's been a really long time for me." He couldn't imagine how long, and it would be humiliating to admit how many years had passed. I then stated, as he was kissing me with a taste of malted whisky on his warm tongue and continuing to undress me, "Perhaps we are moving too fast." But knowing I wouldn't stop. What I couldn't be prepared for was his intensity—his take-charge sexuality. It is what I prefer. I've had to be strong my whole life blazing new trails on my own and survive the unimaginable time and time again; this is one area I don't want to be the take-charge strong one.

I missed alluring, wild, and extended sex. Beyond the fact of never losing desire for hot sex is a yearning to be seen. I'm not the easily understood type or someone most men take time to work their way through the abundant layers to discover all that I am and still hope to be. But not only did my new Turkish friend quickly scan me on the outside, he presented an astute summation of sizing me up where my inner self is concerned. We agreed that we both had an instant attraction and some sort of unexplained cosmic explosion between us.

He could go longer than I needed but I couldn't stop. I'd become numb, numb to my nature—my natural instincts of a lustful hunger. But this was not the plan. I was meant to take an extended stroll of getting to know someone and trust enough to ignite the low flame and my utter fear of sex never being the same again. I said, "I no longer have feeling in my breasts from a double mastectomy and it used to be such a huge turn on for me in foreplay." He kept going and only said, "Do you have feeling down here?" I relented and let the moment be what it was — animalistic sex!

Three hours later, we exchanged numbers. I put his first name in my phone, unsure of how to spell his last name. I promised myself not to become obsessive by seeking a text.

I fully expected the tryst to have been a one-night stand. Dear God, a one-night stand at my age. But a text, I should say, a sext came in.

Gentleman: "I want to see you tonight."

Me: "Really?"

Gentleman: "Yes. You're on my mind and can't wait to see you again… to be inside you again."

Me: "Wow."

Gentleman: "I can come by after I finish up at work around 10:00."

Would I be awake? I'm so used to being in bed early and up early ever since surgery after surgery from sheer pain and exhaustion. I noticed that by getting in bed before 9:00 I could escape the deep loneliness I'd been feeling by getting into bed with Stephen Colbert or videos of amusing animals before going unconscious.

Me: "Ok."

He came through the door. No words. He picked me up, my legs wrapped around him. I silently said to myself, "Oh my God. This is movie sex." In the movies, sex can look so hot. Women are picked up like they weigh nothing, and sex happens against a wall. This was better. There was no wall and there's little wall space in my small abode anyway. I was held in mid-air. I'm tallish and not as skinny as I used to be. He's over six feet and holds me without strain. I was swept up in movie sex and no longer nervous. He slid inside me. The volcano builds and erupts. No words. Just breath.

It had been an achingly long time. I've had a handful of make-out sessions the last several years but little else. This was unexplainable. A fantasy that became real and threw me into the world I'd been missing—a world I thought had been permanently buried.

He continued to engage me in sexting. I was happy to play along. It was temporary. I would be leaving for Italy in a month, and he would soon be going back to his kids and hometown.

The stars aligned though by delivering an unforgettable collision. Our fling continued via sexting in Italy and an occasional visit when he came through town. Sometimes our sexting went late into the night where longing would shoot through me as he described where his hands would land and positions that would take me to sweet rapture.

I realized that what I thought *had* to be a slow, romantic scenario to get me to a place where I could trust someone enough to have sex was not meant to be. Instead, I was catapulted out of my stupor to an awakening—I am still a sexual, sensual woman and the loss of my breasts to cancer cannot take that away.

I accepted the hot sex in my life and the sexting where I was explicitly told what was going to happen next. Another lift in the air, another experience of him taking charge of me, and whispering in the dark while the resident owl made his presence known. We'd lie in bed as he'd sing me a song in his native tongue. He talked about the ancient culture and history of his province. He explained the significance of the predominant color of lapis blue seen throughout the 2,500-year-old walled city. He compared the blue of my eyes to the blue color in the country he left behind. We would speak of poetry. He interpreted a Neruda poem to perfection. And I embraced the moment without thoughts of the future.

I was quiet. He read my mind. "You're ready to go again, aren't you?" I smiled to myself in the dark but didn't utter a word. He said, "Ok tiger, let's go." He had the ability to take me to a sensational place—a place where all dark shadows disappeared, and I drifted to a sublime alternate universe. From that moment on, I was called 'tiger' in every text and sext and when we were together again.

Life presents unexpected and unexplained encounters between a man and a woman, and it doesn't invariably mean it becomes until death do us part. Desire is life's intriguing mystery. Why fantastic sex doesn't necessarily lead to true love, or a wonderful connection doesn't always lead to great love and hot sex will forever remain a mystery. At least I am better at accepting this phenomenon in life but still hold to a thread of hope for a gentle knock on the door presenting ideal love.

SPELL
by Nidhi Agrawal

The body is in a prolonged period of a dry spell,
In the bosom, a tangled web of gold.
At the sight of a water-soaked gravestone,
The skin seethes with jealousy.
Ash of grief, cobwebs of love
In the bosom, a tangled web of gold.

There are many words for grief,
And love.
Between the toes, sands of time,
The sunburst slipping through my fingertips.
The cracks of millions of broken hearts,
Cut a gash through the scorched flesh.
The body is in a prolonged period of a dry
Spell,
In the bosom, a tangled web of gold.

Denude the sky,
I see a penumbra hiding behind the mantle.
The rubicund sun, the sky flushes.
The high shrill screeching cries of the clouds,
The body is a mausoleum of dry spells,
In the bosom, a tangled web of gold.

Love Portrait at Sixty-Five

by Peggy Heitmann

Dreaming,   always dreaming
of shimmering turquoise ocean waves
sparkling at dusk,
singing to me, to us: rush-sush, rush-sush.
Hear our wedding song?
Sensual sea spray leans in to kiss the sand.
Even as night envelops us,
I reach into the heavens
pull a star from the bowl of scintillating darkness
write my name and yours in golden letters
and fling it back into the sky.

United by Metal
by Diana Raab, PhD

At fifteen, my first boyfriend and I
took a chance: kissed on a park bench
under cannabis clouds, and the
jet exhaust near Kennedy airport.

Five minutes into it, and before
either of us were ready to commit,
our metal braces linked us most intimately

as a full moon ascended amidst
our raging adolescent hormones.
We giggled and twisted
into a variety of creative positions,

never seeing that event as a fateful
omen for spending our lives
together—rather laughed about who could have found us
in this hard metal embrace.

On the eve of our seventh-grade dance,
we walked barefoot in Cunningham Park
to kiss and hold each other again,
molded into a contorted position,
like those braces which linked us.

He then placed his blue Sergeant Pepper /jacket
onto my shoulders, and silver /ID bracelet
on my thin wrist.

Once in a while
when I see a man with a beautiful smile
seated on a park bench
or when I peruse social media,
I wonder where David might be now.

A Classic Tale of True Love and High Adventure: A Hot Dragon Tale

by Desiree Ducharme

This is not a sequel to The Princess Bride. For years, I thought it would be. Maybe for years I hoped it would be. I have so many questions. Who kills Humperdinck? Does Inigo become the Dread Pirate Roberts? What happens to Fezzik? Is True Love really that terrible? (*Spoiler: It is.*) Why did you read this? Stay with me. Yes, it is a story about a lost Princess, a Pirate, Friendship and True Love. Yes, there are giants and witches and miracle men and evil Princes. It is a story of Love and of Adventure but it is not Morgenstern, nor Goldman. This story started with them. So, it is with The Princess Bride, the book and my obsession with it, that we will begin.

I'll admit, I saw the movie first and not in the theater. We watched a VHS copy during a sleepover, sometime in the spring of 1988. I can't recall the exact date, neither does Bonnie, but we met Fezzik and Inigo together on the pull-out couch at her parents' house. The right movie selection ripples through a friendship for years. Inconceivable? It's true. From that sleepover we have laughed our way through the pain of existence. For more than thirty years, we've rhymed with peanut, filled out "Hello, my name is" tags with "Inigo Montoya", and shouted "to the PAIN" or "LIAR!!!" at each other during moments of need. I was nearly 10, Bonnie was nearly 9. The Princess Bride became the first entry on the Rosetta Stone of our friendship.

I experienced two great traumas in 1987; I became a middle child, and we moved. New school, new library, new room, new house, new bed, new brother, new everything but me. I was still the old me but was suddenly expected to be something more. At 9, I didn't really have a lot of experience with becoming something other than what I had always been. My sister is

18 months older than me. Meaning when my brother arrived, she just gained a little brother. She didn't have to become something other than what she'd been since I arrived. She had an annoying and instant affinity with our brother. Thanks to this, she was also trusted by adults more readily when it came to handing the baby over. She'd had nine years of practice and was proficient in being bigger than me in every way.

My brother was a monstrously huge baby. He was no Fezzik, but he was top of the scales upon entry. As the lone possessor of the y chromosome in our sibling gang, he automatically took up more space than I ever would. To be fair, I had very little interest in this contradictory usurper of my spot as "youngest child." So it was generally Them, together, basking in the glory of living up to expectations, and Me, beside them, in the shadow of becoming but not quite. It was a small shadow, one They had no intention of casting, but I lived in their shade all the same. Then I met Bonnie. She didn't mind that I was me, that I preferred the shadows, that I brought a book to our first (every) sleepover. I didn't have to be anyone but who I was. We wove a cocoon of acceptance around each other and filled it with laughter and witches and giants.

I was already addicted to reading. Didn't matter what, if it had words, I was reading it. Inigo seemed like a decent fellow; I wanted to read him. This was no surprise to anyone who knew me. I asked the librarian for "The Princess Bride by S. Morgenstern." She sent me to the "G" section. G? I executed an eye roll of epic proportions. She was new. (*She was new to our library but she was not a new librarian. She was a great librarian. She instantly diagnosed my biblio-addiction. She did her best to redirect my selections to age appropriate materials. I would hiss, "Censorship" and she would hiss, "Banned for life." We came to an agreement on this after I checked out and read "A Clockwork Orange" when I turned 10. She would point to a book I might not be ready for in my stack and say, "Burgess." I would ask how old. She would say an age that was a million years away, like 16. I'd roll my eyes and ask, how old for me? She would ask if rolling my eyes made me deaf. She was fun.*) I'd read "The Witches" the previous fall and this librarian had suspiciously large nostrils. I checked the M section. No Princess Bride. I marched to the Gs muttering about censorship just loud enough to raise a single eyebrow from my large nostril-ed nemesis. There it was. It was a mass market with a fancy lady riding a horse on the cover. William Goldman's The Princess Bride. A Hot Fairy Tale. I scoffed, then I opened it to the title page. "The Princess Bride S. Morgenstern's Classic Tale of True Love and High Adventure. The 'good parts' version Abridged by William Goldman." Librarians are never wrong. Tricksy librarians.

I was able to read it twice through before it was due back. I loved it. But what happened? It's titled "The Princess Bride" but has very little to say about her except that she is pretty and dumb, pretty dumb. Which was par for the course. (*Like Barbie, who could do anything, right? My "Barbie 6 O'Clock News Playset" arrived with 'Weather Girl' Barbie. 'News Anchor' Ken was sold separately. Barbie News presented by Ken.*) Inigo was in for a tough go. He had fulfilled his life's pursuit. He'd done it. Revenge accomplished. Would he be satisfied in his life choices? Why was Westley mad at Buttercup for getting engaged (she thought he was dead) when he chose to be the Dread Pirate for at least two years? (*Barbie News presented by Ken: Successful man returns to stop pretty woman from marrying warthog faced buffoon who is trying to kill her. Does she deserve his help?*) She had no choice. (*Barbie News presented by Barbie: Warthog Faced Buffoon holds woman captive for three years. How she survived multiple attempts on her life before escaping a forced marriage to her captor. Tonight at 11.*) But mostly, I wondered about Fezzik. His whole life he was looking for acceptance. He found it with Inigo. Did they stay friends? Did Fezzik get to retire and stop fighting?

Naturally, I asked my librarian. It's their milieu. She said, "Good authors think about telling a story. Good storytellers make you tell yourself one." She said things like this sometimes. You just had to wait a minute and stare blankly. She explained that there is another version because the Goldman was an abridgment. 'The Good Parts' as determined by Goldman. This was scandalous censorship! She knew I'd think so. (*She pointed at "The Handmaid's Tale" in my checkouts and said "Burgess." I rolled my eyes. She swapped it for "Matilda." Since "Matilda" was still new and on a wait list, I allowed it. She was a very good librarian.*) Librarians are never wrong.

Tracking down an original Morgenstern became an obsession. The white whale of my personal collection. It started small. I'd just track down a pre-Goldman edition. Easy peasy. My mother was a champion shopper. She began our training at birth. One Black Friday, we hit four malls in six hours. She could fill whole weeks with discount stores. (This was in the 80s, when there were still ashtrays in the children's dressing room cubicles and possessive apostrophes on buildings.) She can really spend time in antique stores. Swap meets, rummage sales, yard sales will do in a pinch, but the antique store is her favorite playground. Antique stores sometimes have books. While my mom scouted for shiny blue bits from Victoria's reign, I would look for sign of old books.

Book scouting is easy if you know where to look. Used books hide. They are good at survival. It's how they avoid being tossed into the garbage or recycled or used to level furniture. In a general, second-hand environment, the books are hidden in plain sight. Used as décor, to fill space between vintage cast iron pots and Mason jars. They are casually displayed in a basket featuring porcelain clown dolls (aka nightmare fuel), or stacked to elevate recovered glass floats. The trick is to check the corners of the store. The low shelves. The spaces where the forgotten and non-shiny items migrate to. You should also look up, to the top shelves. If there is a rickety staircase leading to a cluttered dusty loft, there will be books up there. They lurk in the high, dry spaces or lie in the musty damp.

Aside from these free-range, somewhat feral used book gathering spots, most antique stores have a small, semi-domesticated book selection. This section is almost always near the back, in close proximity to the bathroom. Usually no larger than one case, sometimes just an old plank across some cinder blocks with pre-ISBN Zane Grey pocket books making a last stand with a ragtag army of Burroughs. When it was time to go, my mom would yell through the store and I would bring my finds to the clerk. I would ask if they had seen any Morgenstern as I placed my leather bound rescues on the glass. They would present a dust jacket-less Nancy Drew and tell me it was a first edition. They were not book dealers. I would forgive them this transgression. My mom would ask if I wanted the "more expensive" book the clerk showed me. I would tell her it was a reprint. The clerk would mumble something about all hardbacks being first editions. We would move on to the next shop.

If I was lucky, there would be a used book dealer renting a space in the same strip mall. Book dealers are a weird lot. They don't follow the rules of retail customer service. In general, they are curmudgeons. Grumpy, irrationally angry at questions, and dismissive. They are addicts who have placed their addiction on display and invited you to walk through the echoes of their pain. I learned you should always approach a used book dealer with caution. They are not motivated by making a sale, they are dragons guarding their treasure.

Children are also terrifying creatures. I was one. It was the only thing I could be considered an expert at. Children are unpredictable at best and usually don't have any money. What's worse is children are almost always leaking or mysteriously sticky. Not a good combination for fragile, paper-based treasure hoards. I am, and always have been, a "Messy Bessy." (*I'm over 40 and all of my clothing is stained, ripped or in some way bear the scars of my chaotic, accident-prone existence.*) At 10, I was a walking hazard to the neat and tidy. I could stain my siblings' clothes from fifty paces. I was a threat to lazy afternoons used book dealers were hoping to enjoy. In short, I was a lot of work, and I was unattended. When you are the physical embodiment of barely contained chaos, you get a lot of practice knowing when you will be asked to leave. Since my goal was to search the hoard for a specific treasure, I learned to tame dragons.

First rule of dragon taming is entering the lair with the respect it is due. If you are chewing gum, stick it to the roof of your mouth. If the door makes a noise, move away from it quickly. Do not bring your siblings. Locate the dragon and acknowledge them. Eye contact or a head nod will be sufficient. For the love of all that is holy, do not engage in conversation before surveying the lair.

Casually survey the lair. Lairs follow a pattern of organization. Look for landmarks: locked cases, brooding space, desk, till, magic barrier to the back room. Where is the locked case? Is it free standing by the front door or part of the desk? Is it behind the desk? If you do not see a locked case, you will need to pay close attention to the stacks, especially those closest to the dragon. If you will pass the locked case before entering the stacks, glance at it but continue past. (Lurking at locked cases right as you come in is like slapping your nana when she brings you a plate of cookies. Nobody is happy. Don't do this.) Are the books within modern? Clean? Signed? Faced out? Organized? Is there just one? Scan the case, then move past. If the case is at or behind the desk, do not approach. (If you do this correctly, there could be cookies in your future.) Glance. Acknowledge. Move with calm silence. If the dragon moves to stand near a specific case that is not locked, this is a warning. Move out of sight for a while or browse the 'children's' section. This will soothe the dragon back to its brooding space.

Assess the content of the lair. How is it organized? How many layers? Has there been an attempt at alphabetization? Are there signs for browsing? Is there another room? Do the books fit the space? Are there books on the floor? If there are no stacks of books on the floor, you may want to leave. Resist. They could be new or have an overly enthusiastic dragon-in-training. It could also be a sign that they've lost their keeper. Is there a format preference? Do they specialize? What is their focus? Once you've figured out their niche, find a way to compliment the dragon. "Oh, what a wonderful selection of mid-century Austen." "Is this the 11th edition of the Encyclopedia Britannica? The bindings are so clean!" Grunts or single word answers mean you are making progress.

If the dragon approaches you, be small and listen. Try not to leak or fart near them. Answer direct questions but do not ask yours yet. Explore respectfully for at least ten minutes. If there are other customers, remain where the dragon can see you and don't interrupt. Dragons appreciate self-sufficiency. Locate your section and browse first. If you make it past the 15-minute mark and the dragon has returned to their brooding space (usually the desk with a book or a stack of books), you can cautiously approach the locked case/desk for a proper look.

Dragons respond best if you approach with an intended purchase. This book is bait. It should be within your price range and be something you want. The dragon will judge you on this selection. So choose wisely. Don't just grab a random 'last chance' book. If you've no interest in it, the dragon will know. (There will not be cookies.) This is where the dragon will let you see their most valuable treasures. Those kept in the locked cases, or better yet, the Private Reserve.

You will have a small window to ask the dragon about your heart's desire. This is generally a space of time from desk approach to till opening. "I didn't see any Morgenstern. I'm really looking for a pre-Goldman Princess Bride, but I'd be interested in any Florinese literature or history." The dragon will scoff or send you back to the stacks with minimal vocalization. Assistant dragons (dragons-in-training) will try to sell you a Stephen King. Dragon keepers will make a comment on your Cabbage Patch Doll belt buckle, take you to the basket of petrified Little Golden Books, and perhaps give you a candy. However, if you've made your approach correctly, your dragon may suggest something from their Private Reserve. In short, cookies.

The Private Reserve is the best of the dragon's hoard. Be prepared, you will not leave the shop with it. However, just knowing it exists, seeing it, maybe getting to hold it… It will be kept close to them at all times, generally in the desk or a box under it. Sometimes they will leave the main chamber and retrieve it from the mythic space known as "the backroom." Depending on the dragon, it may be wrapped. My first pre-Goldman Morgenstern was wrapped. The dragon was ex-military of the Vietnam era. He had a massive beard that was mostly gray. He wore a faded P.O.W. baseball hat that was clearly his uniform now. His hoard was mostly dead generals, Sun Tzu, and Machiavelli. His keeper was a spherical hippie, all patchouli and crochet.

The hoard was located at the end of an antique mall somewhere just within the border of Prescott Valley. There was an abandoned railway station about ten miles north where we'd spent the morning collecting rusted bits of train remains to add to our backyard in California. (Your family is weird too.) My mother had disappeared into the antique mall shortly after lunch. She claimed to be looking for the bathroom. It had been at least two hours. My dad and the dragon swapped service stories as my siblings made an appearance and drew the attention of the dragon keeper. We each received a small piece of hard candy. Then my mother appeared and said the magic words, "There's an open house tomorrow." They all went outside to discuss. I presented my bait book, a well worn copy of "1984."

The keeper coo-ed and asked if I'd seen the C.S. Lewis box set. Knowing I didn't have a lot of time, I boldly asked after the Morgenstern. The dragon scoffed and said there were copies of the Goldman in the discount bin out front. I restated that I was looking for a Morgenstern, not a Goldman. The gray dragon asked for my .50 cents. I handed him my quarters and added, "Goldman is good but I'd like to read the original. It would be a shame if Morgenstern was forgotten." It was manipulative. I know. I was 12 and suffering from extreme withdrawals. It had been almost three whole days without a library or bookshop. This bearded dragon would show me his treasure! The Keeper must have recognized my pain. She casually mentioned "that old bundle" might be of interest. The dragon blew smoke at her but she'd been with him a while and waved it away. He disappeared into the magic realm and returned with a brown wrapped bundle.

He placed "that old bundle" on the glass and opened the fragile paper, carefully exposing the calfskin boards. Neither of us breathed. There it was. It was at least a hundred years old. The front board was detached. The spine flopped horrifically, exposing the threads that held the tome together. The gilt was mostly gone from the fore edge. Just beneath that board were the answers. It was right there.

I felt strange. My mouth was dry. I was starting to tremble. My hands were sweaty. I rubbed them on my shirt. They left brown smudges. I looked at them suddenly (and not for the first time) angry they had failed me in this, my moment of greatest need. I could not touch this book with these disgusting appendages! My sister opened the door and announced that they were leaving. I looked at the dragon, right in the eyes. He saw the struggle within me. Without speaking, he removed the front board and turned the flyleaf. "The Princess Bride: A Classic Tale of True Love and High Adventure by S. Morgenstern." The bottom half of the title page was missing. I would have stood right there and let the dragon turn each page as I consumed it with my eyes. The dragon may have let me, we were kin now. My sister would not. There were tears on my face as she dragged me from the lair. It would be six years before I saw another copy.

***

A lot happens to a kid in the 2109 days between 12 and 18. By September, the once little girls who wove a self-styled cocoon of acceptance around each other emerged as full-fledged pre-teens. This is a dangerous and difficult time for women. We're fragile, yet flexible, eager to find the limits of our malleability. Our bodies expand and lengthen at alarming and completely random rates. We gain knowledge with a terrible cost; life is pain. Our internal organs declare war on comfort. The first battles of womanhood rage within us. We turn on those closest to us. (Especially our parents. Sorry, parents. They knew this would happen. Every month? FOREVER!? It was inconceivable! It remains total bullshit. Sorry, kids.) We learn to weaponize our self doubt and throw daggers of insecurity with surprising accuracy. We toughen our own skin and fabricate our first set of emotional armor. Bonnie was challenged by cherubic curves, all at once. She spent her days in agony as her spine took its time lengthening. I was challenged by sharp edges and stagnation. I spent my days honing acerbic wit and sarcasm. At night, I remained small and in the shadows of becoming but not quite.

Together, we clung to our magic cocoon. We knew it was special even then. As we became, we fused the cocoon's remains to our armor. We added new vocabulary to our private language. We rhymed with peanut. We looked puberty in the face and shouted, "DEATH FIRST!" We knew the secrets of the fire swamp. The trees were lovely. We spent our summers there, and every Wednesday night, and Sunday morning, and every other Friday, and sometimes Saturdays. We built up an immunity to iocane. Even as we turned left into childhood, we could feel The Machine sucking our lives away. In 1994, life took The Machine to fifty. Bonnie (and her family) moved to southwest Washington.

It was an emotional time for us. All of us. In the 2109 days between 12 and 18, a lot happens to parents of women as well. Parents of teenage girls are very much witches and miracle men. Frantically cobbling together miracle pills for every tiny thing. It takes all their energy and time and money. Their offspring fire them (we're still pissed about the whole 'life is pain' situation) and then we show up with the corpse of our childhood and demand a cure. Our parents did their best for us, we were their teenagers. They offered the balm of time and patience. We raged at our inability to control the path of our journey. They calmly presented their miracle pills: phone calls, letters, and visits every summer. Since we were both mostly dead, and had already checked our pockets for loose change, we took them. The chocolate coating was a visit just three weeks after the big move.

We were mid-seize on the Zoo of Teenhood. (*High school is the Zoo of Death. It's filled with angry, semi-feral beasts who become increasingly dangerous the deeper you go. Nothing contained within wants to be there. Only those engaged experiments in pain enter willingly. Only those who can manage their own anxiety can escape the fear within. This is why we fabricate armor.*) Even great fools can see that splitting your forces mid-seize is a terrible idea. We were not great fools, so we strategized how to keep our forces together. I was for dropping out and moving into Bonnie's garden shed. (We were not 'great' fools, merely teenagers and not so good with strategy.) This plan was scuttled on day one. My parents would probably look for me and Bonnie's parents would for sure notice. We moved on.

In the next plan Bonnie would live in my sister's second bedroom. (*You read that right. My sister had two rooms. Her room and the guest room. She had reasons. They were bullshit but she held the title of "First Born" which has its privileges.*) This plan involved some light human trafficking of Bonnie in my carry-on luggage. (*Notes on plane travel and security measures pre-9/11: You could go to the gate without a ticket. Yep, just walk right in. You could also wait at the gate to meet your visitors. This plan was legit and would have worked until our parents noticed.*) My dad was with me on this trip and he was bound to notice Bonnie emerge from my carry-on mid-flight, so that plan was out. I must mention that Bonnie was opposed to running away. She was a big sister and her family had just moved. She could not abandon them. Realizing I could not ask her to, we stopped talking about it. We would just have to make it through but be apart. But not yet, and not always.

We spent a few days locked in her new room speaking our language and reinforcing our defenses. We carefully unpicked our magic cocoon fibers from our too small armor. In the last days of together, the last weeks of heart & logic, we spun a little more until we each had an equal size piece. We were each confident the other would be all right. We buffed our newly re-forged armor with the fabric of our cocoon so it reflected the strength we saw in the other and hoped it would be enough.

My addiction eventually overcame our melancholy. Bonnie was one of the few people who did not view my need to visit a library or bookstore as weird. At home, when I was really in need of a hit, I would just go to the library alone. I needed a ride to the mall and other teenagers. (*There is weird parent logic at work here. One teen, alone, is unsafe. Presumably because on my own I'll be forced into joining a gang if left alone. Two teens are safer. Three or more is the safest, so I always needed at least two others to journey to the mall. Fun fact: Mall security qualifies a gathering of three or more as a 'gang'.*) I had to slip away from the gang to go into bookstores. I would lose social standing by brazenly bypassing the Hot Topic for the Walden's and I did not have much social standing to lose.

Mall bookstores were 'new' bookstores. New bookstores did not hold the same power over me that used bookstores did. Don't get me wrong, new books are great and new bookstores are wonderful. However, I'm an addict. I consume books at an unhealthy rate. New books are prohibitively expensive and only for special occasions. (*Like whenever someone else gives you*

one.) New bookstores have a lot going for them. The booksellers
are knowledgeable and friendly. (*They were not dragons.*) The
basket of Little Golden books is shiny not petrified. They're
clean, tidy, and organized. (*They were not lairs.*) Your siblings
are welcome. They have books but they would not have a Mor-
genstern. (*No treasure.*) Up to this point, my quest was limited
to places I could walk to or antique mall adjacent lairs on family
road trips. I had been limited to the Southwest. I was excited to
meet some PNW dragons. By day three, I ached for it.

It had been 715 days since I'd seen the Morgenstern. I
didn't really understand what happened inside me that day. My
mom noticed something was wrong. She thought it was dehy-
dration or heat exhaustion. My eyes were leaking uncontrol-
lably and I couldn't breathe properly. I tried to describe what I
was feeling but it made even less sense when I used words.

I'd felt a cracking inside me, a fissure. A loosening of tec-
tonic pressure. Something broke, a little, somewhere deep in-
side. A tiny bit of something frightfully powerful escaped. It
surged through me. I felt it swirling around my heart. I felt it
settle into the sulci of my brain. It was euphoric and heartbreak-
ing. It changed me. I noticed the change most when I was
questing for the Morgenstern. I got tiny bursts of happiness
when I entered a lair now. Dragons were easier to tame. Keepers
no longer offered me candy. Hoards were easier to navigate. The
tiny bit of something woke and danced under my skin as I
browsed a promising lair. It guided me. It would pulse in my
brain if I chose the right bait book. It fluttered around my heart
as I spoke with dragons. I thought this was my addiction getting
stronger. This scared me so I tried not to think about it. I was
unable to ignore it on day 715.

I stepped through the door of Powell's City of Books and
would have exploded had my skin not contained me. The tiny
something was instantly awake and moving and everywhere.
This place called to it and it happily raced about within me
looking for a way out. Bonnie felt it too. (We were arm in arm
and I was vibrating.) This was a hoard. An impossibly huge lair!
I detached from Bonnie. I heard her mom say, "two hours," and
I began to search for the dragon. I looked for landmarks. Found

a desk and circled. Then I saw a brooding space. Then another. I was on the other side of the room from the initial brooding space scanning for a dragon, when I stepped through a doorway.

The lair expanded before me. The tiny bit of something constricted inside me, solidified in my stomach and then flew apart. I felt it dust the ridges of my brain. Goose flesh erupted across my skin. I saw a glass case and a desk. I circled this room. I ran into an employee by Dumas. I was so overwhelmed I just blurted out, "Morgenstern!" The swirling around my heart was making me nauseated. This was a dragon! The dragon took me to a shelf. There were three spines of bare shelf between Morgensten and Morgenston. The dragon spoke to me but I was too saturated with endorphins. That's when the second dragon approached.

Then I was in a chair. The words "Parts Department" spun in my vision. Bonnie was soothing the dragons and reassuring them I was fine, maybe just a bit dehydrated. There were four adults, three were dragons, one was an assistant.

I'd never encountered more than one dragon in a lair. Lots of assistant dragons and keepers, but always one dragon. Dragons are possessive. They know what is worthy of their hoard. They train assistants to maintain the hoard, tidy the lair, protect it from constantly leaking womb goblins. They have keepers to, well, keep the dragon alive. (*Keepers play a much more vital role to dragon survival than I knew at this point. I was young and did not understand how debilitating life as a dragon can be.*) This place had keepers and assistants and multiple dragons.

It was a collective hoard. A horde of dragons working together. An assistant dragon handed a book to the first dragon who handed it to me in the chair. I took it and probably said something impressive like, "boop snoot." Bonnie was able to make words happen so she thanked them and moved me out of the room. We bought the book (from yet another dragon!) and went out onto the porch. We sat in silence for a time watching the skateboarders play in the traffic on Burnside. Bonnie asked about the book. I looked at it for the first time. "History of the

Florin Royal Houses compiled and edited by S. Morgenstern"
Inside me, deep in the very core of my being, the fissure splintered. Outside me, I vomited. Bonnie told her mom I had an asthma attack and we rode home in mostly silence. Afraid that I would become undone, I would not return to Powell's for several years.

The book became my first Morgenstern. It was dry and you got a real feel for why he hated royalty. It also made me wonder which royal house Lotharon and Humperdinck were in. I scanned for Hammersmith. It was not listed. My quest continued. We went out to Seaside, to "the Coast" as PacWesters call it. I was having a hard time processing that Bonnie would have to live in such a dreary place. Even their beach was overcast and cold. I suddenly understood why Grunge Rock was a thing and why it could only have been bred in the PNW. The seaside towns had boardwalks, thrift stores, and quite a few lairs. None that would have a Morgenstern but a fair representation of the region. A lot of Herbert, Kesey, and Cleary.

I was relieved that I did not throw up in any of them. Bonnie insisted on coming with me to the first hoard. I'm glad she did. Moral support is vital to the survival of a friendship. (It's a core value.) She didn't know what happened to me either, but she didn't shy away. We had been worried that I'd overdosed, or something. (*If you didn't live through the "D.A.R.E" years, you may not understand. I was still on a waitlist for Trainspotting and was wildly under-informed about drugs.*) Since I was supposed to "Just Say No," I feared telling an adult would prevent me from continuing my quest. The swirling bits had not calmed for two days. I was anxious and snappy. My dad was concerned. (He was the parent of a teenager. He was always concerned.) The PNW dragons soothed the power within me. They recognized my becoming. They knew even if I didn't. By the third shop, I felt more in control. The swirling chaos settled on the inside of me again.

It no longer felt as if it was trying to escape, wildly flinging against every cell. During my success at Powell's, it came on like an explosion or a tidal wave. Like being caught in the wrong spot as a set rolls in, a sudden mountain of water crashing over, into, and through me. Now, it was like a monsoon. A slow building pressure in every pore. I could sense the air pressure change. I could smell the water, I could hear the desert preparing for the deluge. Lightning and thunder precede the flood, but I could see how the landscape would keep dry land under my feet. It still sparked dangerously close to the surface in a promising lair but I could enjoy the ride.

In the final lair of our trip to the coast, I selected a mass market Jurassic Park, Chip Kidd's masterpiece on the cover, and presented it to a middle-aged assistant dragon. Her hair was held in a French twist by several pencils. It was casually messy and practical. I felt an instant affinity towards her. There was an old leather tome open in front of her. Next to her was a stack of photocopies held together by a single metal ring. Post-it notes, like molting feathers, poked out randomly on all sides of the stack. I was going to ask after the Morgenstern but a very different question escaped me, "What are you doing?" She smiled oddly, "My job." She turned the book and showed me the publisher's mark and date. "If this matches the listing in this bibliography, then I might buy it." She handed me the stack of photocopies and pointed at the relevant section.

The vocabulary was unfamiliar. At first, the entry read like gibberish. A collection of sentence fragments. While I read the passage through a few times, she pulled a pencil from her head and made a note on the back of a business card. I asked her several more questions that were not related to the Morgenstern. It was strangely involuntary and I was getting frustrated by my inability to focus. Bonnie waved at me through the window. I was running out of time. "What are you really looking for?" She tossed the life-saver expertly in my direction and pulled me in.

"Inigo…Fezzik…The Princess Bride. A Morgenstern. Have you seen one?" I stammered. I was flushed and my vision blurred momentarily. I was not in control.

"Not for a long while." Her eyes sparkled nefariously. "Where did you see one?"

"Arizona. About two years ago." How could she have

known? My stomach was flipping over on itself.

"Arizona!" She laughed as she finished writing the receipt. It was a warm laugh. A lock of hair freed itself and framed her right eye, a visual parenthesis. She placed a copy of "ABC for Book Collectors" by John Carter on top of my bait book. "You'll need this, eventually. Promise you'll wait a few years." I slid the last of my savings across to her. I didn't notice the business card tucked expertly between the flyleaf and end page of the Carter until I was on the plane home.

Valerie's Old Books & New Spells
Est.1603
Salem, Ma.
On the back, written in pencil: *Ask for Val. Don't mention Goldman.*

I could feel the strange power pulsing between my fingertips through the card. The card itself felt strange. It wasn't card stock. It was thin and warmed slightly as I held it, like skin. Skin I was familiar with. There was a light crackling sound, like embers. Possibly, the sound was coming from me. The longer I held it the less familiar it became. Less familiar, yet increasingly intimate. I knew this flesh by touch. I knew it deep, at the core of myself. It was entirely too much. I tucked it and the book away.

I intended to tell Bonnie about it. However, every time I tried, something distracted me. We were in separate pits of despair. Our forces were divided. Bonnie met a boy. Then another. There were Princes hunting near her. There were balls and concerts and castles on her horizon. I was trying to find suitable camouflage for my growing addiction to the written word. I wanted nothing more than to be left alone with a horse named Horse and the collected works of Hugo and Dumas. The only thing I wanted on my horizon was a pre-Goldman Princess Bride. I wanted it so much, I became reckless with the hearts of others in pursuit of my goal.

Case in point: Bobby. I spent my Senior year dating Bobby. Bobby had eyes like the sea and hair the color of sunlight in Fall. He was only a year younger than me but two grades behind. He was poor and perfect. He was my social shield. I was able to opt-out of all forced social participation (dances) because I had a boyfriend and thus no longer needed to attain one. Brilliant. Or it was, until Bobby said he loved me about two weeks in. I liked Bobby, a lot. He was kind, empathetic, and generally up for whatever. Like spending endless hours being ignored by his girlfriend as she hunted through the musty lairs of SoCal dragons muttering about long dead translators and missing colophons. Bobby was a Westley. I was not his Buttercup. I had a strong feeling I wasn't anyone's Buttercup. The kindest thing to do was to end it. I did. The week I graduated. It was terrible, all of it. I did not mean to use him or break his heart. I had no intention of breaking my own. I was quite honest but sometimes hormones and romantic ideals make one deaf to truth. All the choices we make come at a cost. Life is pain, kids.

Goldman cuts large parts from Buttercup's story. He does it with the phrase, "What with one thing or another, three years passed." In fairness, the education of women has always been tossed aside as boring. Fictional heroines like the Protagonist Princess often have a space of time redacted from their history. We tend to avoid talking about how little girls become women, how common becomes uncommon. How truths become fiction. Like Buttercup, we learned a lot even though our education could be described as nothing more than intense drudgery with a side of general Gen-x angst. We're going to skip it.

What with one thing or another, two years passed.

I made my first trip to the east coast in the late summer of '96. On the third day, I stumbled across the Brattle Bookshop. They were closing up for the night and the dragon was out but the assistant told me there might be a Morgenstern outside. (*Yep, OUTSIDE. Brattle has a lot next to their shop with carts of 'last chance' books. It's a veritable dragon playground in a parking lot. There are also cabinets out there. Year-round. In Boston. Where it snows. It is amazing and terrifyingly reckless.*) She took my name and said she'd pull it and hold it at the desk until end of business the following day. This was not procedure but we were kin. She warned me that it was in very poor condition but had at least one more read in it. Our conversation ended with her passing me an application.

This was happening quite a lot in hoards and even new bookstores. On this trip to Boston, I'd been passed four applications and a business card. (*Just in case. In case of what? In case you change your mind.*) I would explain that I was just visiting. The dragon or assistant or keeper would smile oddly and say, "Whatever gets you through." I didn't understand it.

The maybe-Morgenstern turned out to be an actual Morgenstern and it was The Princess Bride. It was a reprint from the 20s. An English translation bound in red cloth that faded to a dusky rose at the spine. A white Dewey Decimal number (813.54) screamed tacky at the base of it. The only external indication that it was ex-lib. The deckled edges were darker in spots, stained with 70 years of reader's remains. The top fore-edge claimed the book for "Stevens" in black marker. Corners swollen from years of damp, brown fans spreading between the bumped away fabric. The flyleaf and frontispiece were missing. The boards were nearly detached at both the front and back. A mid-century librarian at Mather Elementary attempted a repair at some point. The possibly-not-always brown strip of binding tape, cracked and brittle with age, was splitting in places. Thin threads stretched across the gaps like desperate rope bridges across a canyon. I wonder if it was the same librarian who eventually stamped it 'Withdrawn.' Cradled in the palm of my hand, I let the pages slide past my thumb until they revealed the broken binding in three places. (Pages 158/159, 430/431, 602/603.) All the pages appeared to be intact. The card pocket was missing but the telltale grey adhesive square remained on the inside of the backboard. Jane received it at Christmas 1962. Ben on his birthday in 1970.

I paid $2.50. The assistant dragon wrapped it with care and handed it over. I practically ran from the shop. I had to get out before the tears escaped. After six years of searching, the answers were in my possession at last. The economics of questing are unbelievably simple. The emotions follow no pattern whatsoever. I didn't attend my scheduled lectures that afternoon. I sat in a café and began reading. At 6pm, I called Bonnie. She was waiting for the Prince to return from a hunt. She began reciting the protocol for Waiting-for-Prince but I interrupted her.

"I found one. A Morgenstern. A Princess Bride." I wondered if she could hear the imminent existential crisis behind my rushed confession.

"Really? That's great!" There was a momentary pause. "A reading copy?" Her tone was cautious. She was always a good listener. She knew I was struggling.

"Yes. I own it."

"And?" She knew I'd already begun reading it. She was expecting a full report. I thought about my answer. In truth, it was rather dull and slow going. Before I could articulate my disappointment, my long distance card ran out. *You have one minute of call time remaining.* "I'm out of minutes."

"Oh! Call me Sunday. I don't have plans with the Prince but we might attend Homecoming! I sent you the details. You'll have three letters when you get home."

"I'm flying Sunday…" *You are out of minutes.* The line went dead. This is when I realized the stillness inside me. Given my reaction six years ago, I felt achingly hollow. Not at all what I was expecting. The storm within me never broke. No river of power filling the canyons of my soul. No flashes of light. No deafening thunder. Just this still silence. The line inside me dead as well. Perhaps I'd outgrown my childish fantasy. The treasure, now in my possession, felt like nothing more than $2.50 of slowly decaying fibers.

I wandered the cobbled streets of Beantown contemplating the nothingness within me. I visited the bones of American legends turning to dust side by side with the bones of ordinary people. I visited the bones of ordinary people and wondered if this was all there was. A small star in the center of a busy intersection marked the spot where ordinary people killed each other several centuries ago. I watched several tourists risk their lives to take photographs of it between light cycles. Their camera flashes a strange reminder of the absence in my bones. In less time than you would think, I was lost down an alley and found myself in Commonwealth Books. I felt a low-grade buzzing in my feet as I flipped through their ephemera.

Commonwealth had a classic Old 'New World' Book smell even though their fixtures were clearly new. Lived-in leather, dry cotton, and parchment filled my lungs. It gently rolled along the inside of me, soothing the hollow ache with every breath. I felt it opening capillaries. The low-grade buzzing ran up my legs and ended in my fingertips. The lair was organized, yet organically haphazard, like moving day. The point on moving day where you can't tell if someone is preparing to move out in a hurry or is taking a really long time moving in. An old dragon was brooding behind a fortress of wood pulp, hemp, and leather. We made eye contact. He smoked lightly out one nostril when his eyes came to rest on my battered Morgenstern. "I picked it up at Brattle this morning." Hoping to strike the right tone. A tone that was an acknowledgment of the horrendous abuse the tome had taken and that I was not the abuser, but its new, forever home. Some dragons are particular about what you bring into their lair. He held out his hand. Rather than hand it to him, I held it up higher and pulled the receipt up so he could see it. I was surprised to find that I was reluctant to turn it over.

The dragon relaxed slightly. He appeared to steam evenly from both nostrils. "You might be interested in the Guilderian maps in the case. Back wall on the right. Third drawer." I nodded my thanks. I couldn't have spoken. The room was beginning to spin slightly and my vision blurred. The familiar pulsing sparks burst happily around my heart. I felt tears welling. I was not dead inside! I mastered the wave with measured breaths taking care to finish browsing the ephemera basket. My fingers brushed the cellophane wrapper on the final item in the basket. An intense wave pulsed through my hand. I pulled the item without looking at it and made my way to the map case.

There were Guilderian maps in the case. They were all a bit too modern for my taste. There was an excess of smoke lingering in the corner. I fanned it away using the piece of ephemera in my hand. The not-so-tiny something was running amok through my chest and arms. I looked at the item.

It was a charcoal sketch on possibly parchment depicting a sword fighter in the courtyard of a mission. It was a rough outline at best. I inspected the edges. It had been bound at some point. The regular holes and brightness of the left side suggested something more. I noticed the smoke blurring my vision again. It was coming from me. I bought the sketch, casually asking the dragon if he knew its provenance.

"I think this was one of Val's." He flipped through a slip case of business cards. Dragons often use old slip cases for filing or storage of important documents. Almost every lair has an old Lord of the Rings box filled with pencils or rubber bands or blades of various sizes. You can sometimes divine a hoard's focus based on the slip cases-turned-desk accessories. He extracted a card and slid it into the bag with my purchase. I left the close comfort of Commonwealth for the cobblestone alley. It was the first time in over six years that I left a bookshop without asking after a Morgenstern. I was once again standing in a shadow of becoming but not quite.

Spontaneous Combustion
by Gerard Sarnat

Foot stomp, run your mouth
feel-bad confetti romance
turd terrorism
in vast Delhi garbage heaps:
peeps burned, scrounge to earn livings.

This morning

by Anna Laura Falvey

I felt it
somewhere behind
my eyes
when I woke
up that I'd be late
to work.
I had a bad dream –
I've been
having bad dreams
the past few nights,
but in this one
I was alone
and confused. When I woke
up I also felt alone
and confused
but then I moved
my foot slightly
and I felt Sarah's calf,
warm
and firm
and still. When
she woke
up she told me her dream,
which was also bad,
and I told her mine.
She stayed
in my bed
while I got ready,
watched me pace
between my closet
and my dresser
deciding what to wear,
watched me strip
out of the shirt
I slept in
and step into
a fresh pair of underwear,

hook closed my bra.
I am not
used to her, soft
and languorous
in my bed,
and I felt
my heart expand
with my lungs
as I breathed
deep in.
I sat down
cross legged
in front of my mirror
and she sat
down behind me,
tucking her legs
under my knees.
I tapped
concealer under my eyes,
pressed springpink
blush to my cheeks
while she lifted
the hem of my sweater,
her lips drifting
along my back, hands
firm set
on my hips. The sound
of the church bells
floats through
my half open window
with the April chill.

Homemade

by Rin Stone

"Homeless"
your sign says,
pointed at me,
your home five years previously.

I swear the floors have never been the same since you left.
No matter how hard I scrub the decomp stains cling to the old
wood.

When I was Katie, you made her your home.
You changed her tiling, her lighting, her fixtures.
I would wake up looking out through my windows hoping that
you would like what you saw.
Hoping that the changes you made helped me be a home better
suited to your needs.

I begged my mother to let you move in and,
told her how awful your mother was,
told her how none of this was your fault.
There is still plenty that I don't think is your fault.
I don't blame you for wanting to rearrange my furniture to
resemble the only home you've ever had.

So she let you move in,
and your vines grew through me,
rearranging my mostly vacant space,
and pushing out the few things I meticulously placed.

The new paranoid delusions,
I mean,
the new couch isn't exactly what I'd pictured and…

The meth,
I mean,
the flowers on the table aren't really my taste and…

The rent money disappearing,

I mean,
marble countertops aren't really practical are they?

And on.
And on.
And on.
Until I look in the mirror.
I see your vines shrouding her small frame,
pulling her into the floorboards.
You have trained her not to fight it,
and she didn't.

I don't know if I believe in reincarnation but,
Katie and I have both lived here,
and I've spent a long time cleaning up your mess.

Like I said,
There's still decomp on the floor.

But I've trimmed the vines away,
even though I still cough some up from time to time.
From when she lived and breathed you.
From when you lived and breathed in her.

I'm not a shelter anymore,
but I hope you find your way.

Time
by Lynette Esposito

If time
were my lover,
I would never be alone.
but
She said let's just be friends.

and so
as things go,

I grew old and time stayed young.
When the end came near,
she parted ways with me.
I no longer needed a friend like her
and she no longer needed me.

Still, as I close my eyes
to dream or not,
her days with me went well.

Emmanuella's Revenge

by K. B. Thomas

Dear Emmanuella,

I just put the baby down for his nap and had to write to you right away. What you must be feeling, trapped on that leaking pirate ship with all those rats and bad food – and Cole so far away from you! Not to mention the pirate leader who, when I last saw him, was on his way down to your cabin with rape in mind. I have the laundry to sort, so this is going to be a quick letter.

Please, beautiful Emmanuella, please take a quick look around that dark cabin and find some sort of weapon – there's got to be a knife to stab him with or a forgotten black powder gun in one of those sea chests. I know Cole will still love you no matter what happens, but I think it would be better for your relationship if you gave a good fight. Perhaps you can take a few minutes to mix a poisoned concoction from the small box of medicines mentioned ten pages or so ago? Just a thought.

Much love,
Nadine

Dear Emmanuella,

Brad's giving the baby his bath, so I thought I'd take a moment to write to you. I never, never thought you'd jump from that ship and swim to the tropical island that was mentioned in passing conversation four chapters ago! There you are now, your hair a salty mess and your dress in tatters, peering through the vegetation at the English regiment that is stationed there for the sole purpose of stringing up pirates. The English, Emmanuella! If only you could go to them for food and shelter! If only you hadn't been unjustly branded on your left shoulder as an English criminal in the previous book! Then you'd be safe, and with the regiment's handsome captain. What are you going to do now? Thank goodness for your extensive knowledge of tropical vegetation. You can hide for a few days, avoiding that poisonous berry mentioned in the second chapter. Who would have thought that living with those nuns for three months, studying botany, would come in so handy?

But what are you going to do about clothing? How is Cole going to find you?

Sorry to go on and on, but I mostly wanted to write to tell you to watch out for the small group of French criminals hiding about two miles from you. They recently escaped from a Bahamian clove plantation. They're a rather desperate bunch.

Well, I have to clean up the dinner dishes now. Take care.

Love,
Nadine

Dearest Emmanuella,

The baby's a little fussy today, so this will have to be short. What a lucky woman you are! To find your beloved cousin Victor among the group of French criminals! Imagine recognizing him after so many years because of his club foot! Good to know that you are finding men's trousers so much more comfortable than those gorgeous gowns and their twelve yards of material. I also find pants more comfortable, especially when vacuuming. Now that you're clothed and fed, you can concentrate on Victor's plan to overthrow the English regiment and gain control of the island. You do know that if you participate in the attack on the English you could be captured and sent to Australia. How will Cole find you there? But I suppose a man like Cole would travel halfway around the world to reach you. Even though Victor promises he'll take you to Kingston to find Cole, and he looks as though he means it, do you trust him? I know, I know, what choice do you have?

Things here are fine. Brad and I have to go car shopping this weekend. Just thinking about it gives me a headache, but I'll be glad to get out of the house.

Love,
Nadine

Dear Emmanuella,

Between the baby's colic and your capture by the English, I didn't sleep at all last night. Forgive me if this is a little incoherent. You were absolutely fantastic there on the beach, dueling with the captain of the regiment. I am so sorry that there was a full moon and he saw your branded shoulder. If not for that, I'm sure you would have made it to the waiting longboat to escape with Victor. At least the English captain has the good sense to see how lovely you are; you must use him in some way to make your escape. I'm sure Cole will understand. Things haven't always been perfect for the two of you, but you always manage to forgive the mistakes, the small indiscretions.

I know that you love Cole – your fans are told that again and again – but really, after four hundred pages without seeing each other isn't it hard to stay faithful and true? I hate to tell you this, because you've got troubles enough right now, but Cole has been shanghaied onto a whaling vessel, sailing out of Martha's Vineyard. He won't see land for another two years.

Brad and I did find a car we like but can't agree on how much to spend on monthly payments. I'll keep you posted.

Love,
Nadine

Dearest Beautiful Emmanuella,

This will have to be short as Brad found my letters to you and is taking me to see a doctor this afternoon. He hid "Emmanuella's Revenge" from me but I bought an e-copy and downloaded it to my phone.

Imagine having the book taken just as you are boarding the ship that will carry you and the other women prisoners to Australia! Why, oh why did your English captain have to eat those berries? Now, with no protector, you're once again a prisoner of the Crown. The only good news that I can see is that Cole is also sailing the high seas, and is bound to find you. All the world's oceans can't keep you two apart! It says so on the back of the book.

I shall never forget those last pages of "Emmanuella's Revenge" as you took the sick and broken women prisoners and roused them with your beauty and eloquence. I am altogether behind your planned rebellion. With your expert nursing, those women will soon be able to fight for themselves and toss the sailors overboard. And then, Emmanuella, with your own ship, the world will be yours!

I can't wait to read "Emmanuella the Pirate Queen"!

Love,
Nadine

kiss me
by Livio Farallo

so i have found out,
eyes drenched are
nothing more
but soft interruptions
in sorrow. and
i am a
vacant shout
from the breath
of a mountain;
skin pulled tight
over weathered rock,
over gasps of wind.
and in puffs of rain,
like cancer digging
a tree's roots,
i am never-ending.

i'm sick to death
of the adolescents' hormones:
the world's
reasons for staying in robes;
its religion spilling down slopes.

sick to death

from the flower's color
in the city morning
to its brown
at midnight.

i am sick to dirty death
without another step in your suburban mud.

and interruptions
in the flaky pastry of the sun
are what my feet would be
where they dance

high, stirring up sweet
fillings like a whole cherry pie
around your lips.

but i am softness there
unspeaking and lasting
beyond a toehold,
lasting beyond the loud
confection of a touch.
and my heels
as they dig in
are like badgers
at the twinge
of your disappearing smile.

since then
by Francesca J. Sidoti

we have kept our pantry full of deep kisses
stolen maid-butler style hugs meant for spouses.
we have kept our shame voices low on the phone,
a better picture than the real thing. whispers
make weakness clear. We are cracked full in our
shells. Made for everyday wear-and-tear, uniforms
cover it well. I am not the same as before.
please let me erase the tape, scroll back surveillance cams.
we serve separate households. and our beds
have forgiven us in our sleep.

Inducing the Light
by Nam Hoang Tran

On Those Moments
by Ranjith Sivaraman

A purple flow with a tint of pink

A musk rose fragrant honey
A long wild strumming of guitar
What else she can say
More than these
of those moments.

Photo Taken in Times Square, 2010

by David de Young

It's been on my desk since I started this job, that framed
print of the selfie we took in Times Square –
September 2010, our first date – the Golden Arches,
and the red stripes of TGI Fridays behind us,
me in a light-yellow shirt, you in a turquoise scarf and a
necklace you still have. Glasses we've both since replaced.

I don't notice it always, but today I do, recalling
the different time and country in which it was taken.
Then, we did not know our future – my moving, our children,
the unending mettle required of us all – but clearly, we knew
something, my arm around your neck, hand on your shoulder,
my thumb pressing your upper arm, holding on.

A Romance in 300 Words
by Sarah Denison

1. *Cempasúchils*

I am whispering in the room of my heart.
Do you hear me?

When my skull tingles,
When you cook eggs in the morning,
When I wake in the night and you're still asleep but your hand
reaches for my thigh anyway?
When we kiss in the parking lot and someone whistles and I get
mad but you just
Laugh?

When I look at you and wonder exactly when I lost the will to
look away?

Maybe when I give you marigolds and watch you rip the petals
one by one -
>   *she loves me*
>   *she loves me*
>   *she loves me.*

2. How to Apologize

"What?"
"I said, are you even listening to me?"
"Woah, are you mad? What did I do?"
"The least you could have done is texted to say you were gonna
be late."
"What is with you and texting? You're so needy."
"I'm not needy. It was inconsiderate."
"Why are you making such a big deal about this?"
"I'm not. I just want-"
"What?!"
"I just want you to say you're sorry."
"Fine. I'm sorry if you felt I was being 'inconsiderate.' Happy?"

"No! That's not a real apology."
"Jesus! You're so dramatic! Fuck this shit."
"Wait! Come back! I'm sorry."

3. *Erigenia Bulbosa* (Harbinger of Spring)

You used to call me "delicate flower." I thought you were
teasing, like when I called you "grumpy." But now I think that's
how you wanted me. Because if I were delicate, I would be
easier to bend.

But what you don't know about flowers is that the most delicate
ones – the ones that bloom in early spring – are not delicate at
all. They are hardy. And clever. Before anyone else gets a
chance, they push through frost-hardened ground – beat the
forest to the sunshine. They gulp it down. They drink their fill,
make love to the bees, and survive.

for you
by BEE LB

each day grows longer in accordance with desire
to be closer to you; time bends towards want
as do we all.

the sun traces across your lips and were i
with you, i'd not hesitate to give in
to the urge to lick light from your skin.

when i think of how often the sun gets to
touch your gentle body, i can't help
the jealousy that reaches through me.

when i feel the sun stretching
across my cheeks, i can't help but to feel it,
a shared kiss across distance.

when i reach for your hand i am asking
for your heart and with each resounding
touch, i grow closer in devotion.

spanning the length of distance, begging
for closeness— i find something entirely new;
the sound of need stretching from your tongue

to mine, stringing us both together. i can't help
but gorge myself on desire, this love fashioned into
need; stretched into something that can fit us both within.

Chance or Destiny: A Personal Essay

by Helga Gruendler-Schierloh

Sufficiently bilingual and completely broke, I was finally back in my native Germany.

After having spent an entire year as an "Au Pair" in London, UK, to mold my school English into an employable skill, I was still not all done with my language studies.

My next step was to add French, the language of love, to my linguistic repertoire of foreign grammar and vocabulary. That meant lining up a Parisian family who would trust me with taking care of their kids and pets, and possibly with some other household duties. But to be able to set my plan in motion, I first had to get a hold of some sorely needed cash. Of course, getting a job seemed the most logical solution to that problem.

One hot summer afternoon, after enjoying the buzzing downtown activities of my beautiful, two-centuries-old home town in the foothills of the Bavarian mountains, I was bone-tired and ready to head back to my parents' home. On my way to the train station, I decided to stroll through the intriguing, tunnel-like passage adjacent to the local newspaper.

To my left, the narrow enclosure donned a dismal, blank cement wall. However, to my right, the exterior of the old building was awash in a sea of paper slips pinned and taped to it.

As I glanced curiously across that huge, black-and-white chaos of ads, announcements, and other miscellaneous messages, two words suddenly jumped out at me.

"Bilingual Secretaries" headlined the message of a known, local manufacturing company seeking bilingual secretarial support for a German-American program. I eagerly copied down the contact number and, a few days later, I succeeded in securing an interview—and a job.

I planned on staying with that company for the few months still remaining, to the end of that year, before heading to France. I pinned high hopes on three languages to launch a career as a translator, interpreter, or possibly both.

Christmas neared, and as I was agonizing over giving my notice to quit, everything suddenly changed when a whispered rumor circulating through the company caught my attention. Since ours was a bilateral program between the United States and Germany, people of both nationalities were working together at our facility. But now it was apparently time for a role reversal—with the Americans returning home and taking a number of Germans with them.

I quickly decided to wait and see who would or wouldn't be chosen to go. And, not too much later, I signed a two-year contract that would allow me to explore the United States on a free or rather "most expenses paid"- ticket. France just had to wait a while. I could always tackle that country and its language later on. At least that's what I thought at the time.

I found the USA fascinating, and at the same time quite different from how I had imagined it. I kind of expected every big city to be filled with lots of skyscrapers. However, much to my surprise, the metropolitan area where I was to live and work for the next two years didn't have many tall buildings. It also happened to be flat as a board. Besides, on the day I landed there in the middle of June, it was blistering hot—which made me wonder if I had arrived in the tropics.

However, I enjoyed checking out my new surroundings as well as traveling to Florida, New York, Washington D.C., and Mexico.

Toward the end of my second year, one of my German co-workers and I decided to attend a Halloween celebration that was staged within our work environment. We had the address, wore plenty of makeup, but weren't sure about the BYOB printed on our invitation.

Arriving at the party, we soon figured out what it meant. Everyone but us had obviously heeded the advice to "Bring Your Own Bottle."

The gathering was also sparsely attended and anything but lively. Faced with nothing to drink and to do, my friend and I decided to leave. Suddenly the door swung open and two young men entered. I instantly spotted the beer in one of the new-comer's hands. Like a lightning rod I was at his side, pointing at the brew. Laughing, he handed me the entire six-pack.

"Here you go," he said. "I don't like that stuff anyway, but since we were already running late, that's all I could grab in a hurry."

My friend impatiently pulled on my sleeve. "Hey, what about getting out of here?"

"In just a minute," I told her, holding up the bottles. "We are actually in pretty good shape now to stay a little longer."

I don't recall what she ended up doing after that. I for one was busy chatting with our generous booze donor. He was really cute, and the alcohol must have further enhanced my vision. In any case, I was quite taken with him—and the same thing seemed to apply in reverse.

When it was time to go home, he asked me for my phone number—and I was happy to give it to him. But when he didn't even bother writing it down, my excitement instantly waned.

Oh, well, I thought, pegging him as one of those dazzlers who merely pretend to be interested. I consoled myself with having had a really good time for one evening anyhow.

Days later, my office phone rang. It was my Halloween flirt, asking me out. Amazed that he had retained my number, I agreed to meet him for dinner. Our first date went well—and so did the many others that followed. And before long, we were in love.

A few months later, my contract was up—and he was clas-sified A-1. So, in spite of how we felt about each other, it was time to part—with a mutual promise to stay in touch.

I went home to my country—with my plans of going to France still being very much on the backburner. He was about to be drafted and possibly sent off to war. The likelihood of the two of us ever meeting again seemed rather remote—if not impossible. As once before, I took comfort in the wonderful time we had been able to spend together.

But fate obviously wasn't done with us yet.

My returning household items were still at sea when the bilingual administrative assistant of one of our affiliates in the United States needed to be replaced. Of course, I was keen on going back. About the same time—because of his unique employment status—my American love was granted a deferment from military service.

Two months later, I was on a plane again—anxiously anticipating HIM. Although we ended up in a long-distance relationship for a while, at least we were on the same continent and in the same country. Just before my contract was to expire this time, we got married.

My company transferred me back to the city of his residence and then—one bureaucratic step after another—I immigrated to the United States.

I have been here ever since—because of two words peering out at me from the midst of a huge paper jungle. Was it all mere chance, or is there actually such a thing as destiny?

Oh yeah, and France?

My husband and I eventually visited Paris for one day, taking a sightseeing tour through the city. Needless to say, that was hardly conducive to mastering French.

So, for whatever it is worth, my language of love turned out to be English.

My mother has a singing voice you'd invite to your wedding

by Junix Seraphim

Maybe once I had a voice
on its way to being
like hers
But that was before
I changed it
Learned to speak
rattle chest less
nasal
Unlearned girlhood
I coo, "Good, good,"
to the man from Grindr
Cupping the back of his bald
soft head
He says he really wants
to come but really
He is asking permission
When he comes in me I call him
good boy. It is the first time
I call him anything

Maybe the secret to men
is we all yearn to be mothered
Practicing mommy kink &
You ever think Oedipus
was onto something?

Beloved
by Justin Ratcliff

Do not hide your face from me

Let your light touch me

Dearly beloved

Hear unto my plea

Let not any barrier

Come betwixt us

May we be

Forever entwined

Till the celestial bodies

Turn to dust and ash

May our hearts' tantric enigma

Be a fire that surpasses all bliss

May hell's heat pale

When compared to our

Splendor

Figurehead

by Anna Laura Falvey

The sun glints a wicked light
on the whitecaps today.

the landline shimmers,
the quivering mouth

of a lovesick sailor who keeps
his girl's likeness folded up

and pressed to the inside of
his cheek like chewing tobacco.

the fabric of my dress clings to
the shape I make, long like a breath

arched like the branch of something
ancient. The day is not as long

as the one before – the sun sets earlier
with each pass. When the moon hangs

high above me held in the shapeless arms
of the clouds, a hand slips itself into mine

from the bough above my head. My love's
cheek presses to mine, her body draped

over the ship's bow. The drift of her hair
in the wind disturbs the ambit, goldbrown

curls braid with the horizon. I wish, as I do
each night, I could turn my head to meet her.

Instead, we watch the water together,
feel the swell of the ocean's breath below.

Disappointed for the Ages

by Nam Hoang Tran

Nature

by Lynette Esposito

In the morning
before it rains,
nervous blue water
kisses the sandy shore line
until a dark storm interrupts
this noisy love affair.

Then all is still.

The water sleeps--
its silver face serene.

Here Comes Trouble

by Cynthia Close

I have sexual amnesia when I try to remember those most intimate moments with Pete. Sex had lured him to me, but my attraction to him was more conscious. A calculated thing. Once, after we had been married about six years, I suggested we consider having other consensual sexual relationships within the context of our marriage. Marge and Dave were an attractive couple with a little girl about our daughter's age. We were close friends. I felt an underlying erotic tension when we were all together and I guess I had them in mind when I made this suggestion. Pete fumed. He nearly popped a gasket. It was the last time this idea was brought up. Perhaps the fact that he was cheating on his wife when he started dating me came back to haunt him.

Construction on my Fort Point studio continued. I was also working part-time as a gallery director at the BVAU (Boston Visual Artists Union) gallery on Washington Street in the heart of Boston's Old North End. The organization moved there when we lost our luxury digs in Government Center. It was a great job for me. Flexible hours. I shared the position with my good friend and fellow artist, Renee. She and I each had a desk a few feet from each other but facing the gallery entrance so we could see everyone who came in. Some days we would be there together planning exhibitions, meeting other artists, or writing the grants that helped to keep the whole operation afloat. My lawyer friend Frank was still very active with the group. He donated tons of time and expertise to our cause, which was the advancement of artist's rights. Frank was also looking to date cute women.

On a warm, languid, city-summer afternoon Renee and I were both sitting at our desks. The gallery windows were open since this turn of the century building lacked air conditioning. There was a bulletin board by the main entrance where we posted notices of available loft space, exhibition opportunities, jobs, etc. I tended to be more gregarious, so greeting visitors and trying to get new members to join the organization fell to me. On this day in 1980, I glanced towards the door, thinking of nothing in particular. A slender, broad-shouldered man appeared at the top of the stairs leading to our second-floor space. His wavy, slightly graying hair caressed the collar at the open neck of his casually wrinkled pale blue cotton shirt. He stood there, relaxed, a bit of the weathered cowboy look about him, scanning the bulletin board. He turned his head and looked my way. Deeply set eyes, shrouded in shadow gripped my attention. I rose from my desk like I was levitating.

Renee stared at me and mumbled, "Uh-oh, here comes trouble."

He's a sculptor. Tanned and just returned to Boston from a residency in Roswell, New Mexico. He's looking for studio space. His name is Robin. I am blinded by him. I immediately regret the shapeless, sack-like but cool and comfortable dress I pulled from my closet to wear that morning, thinking only of the workday ahead.

It was part of my job to assist artists looking for a suitable studio/workspace.

"Can I help you?" I asked.

We both smiled. He knew at that moment the multiple meanings inferred by my question. The rest was a dance. He needed temporary space immediately while he looked for something more permanent. I happened to know about an available loft in a building close to the gallery; I gave him the contact information, we chatted for a bit, and then he left. Renee looked at me shaking her head.

Flushed, sweating, giggling, I blurt, "He is beautiful."

The next day he returned to thank me. The space I suggested would suffice for him. He was using it as a working studio while living for the short term in a friend's apartment on Newbury Street till he found a combination live/work loft big enough to accommodate his stone carving. He let me know he would be in his new, temporary space, working to complete a piece he brought back from New Mexico, and he'd be happy to show me some things if I felt like stopping by later.

I had never in my life gone looking for a man, gone to his place to search him out, to see him, to know him. That day, I went to find him. I was familiar with the building, an 1890's red brick, former furniture factory behind a similar building that housed the gallery where I worked. I entered the wide arched stone entrance and took the stairs up to the third floor. Most of the building was empty. All was quiet. I hesitated but reached out to tap on his door, feeling like Alice, about to fall down the rabbit hole. A youthful knowing voice, as though I was expected, said simply, "come in."

His studio is flooded with the raking light of late afternoon sun. His back is to me as he seems to be working on a large, white, plaster relief propped up on an easel. It is a contemporary version of *The Three Graces*, simultaneously classical and of our time. I'm impressed. I'm standing behind him, looking over his shoulder. He slowly backs up a step, in silence, like a dancer in a dream sequence. He's wearing a worn, short sleeved, white T-shirt that now exposes the well-honed muscles of his upper arms. The tips of my breasts just graze his back. I am acutely aware of every cell and pore in my body. Saying nothing, he keeps gently pressing backward. I can't move. I think I may die. I'm about to swoon. He turns to face me. The spell is suddenly broken. His broad mouth curves slightly up in a gentle smile. He looks down at my feet; they are bare, in thin, strappy sandals.

Looking back up to my face he says, "I need a model for feet for a life-sized figure I'm working on. Are you available?"

The thought of someone wanting to use my feet as a model for a piece of sculpture takes me aback. I've never thought of my feet as being particularly attractive. I'm suddenly self-conscious.

"Do you think they're good enough?" I ask, slightly incredulous.

"I wouldn't have asked if I didn't think they would work," he says.

He explains he is trying to finish a large, female figure, a limestone carving he started in New Mexico, but the feet are giving him trouble, he needs a reference.

I'm intrigued. "How do we proceed?"

I knew the studio we were standing in was only temporary. He'd already found a permanent loft on Melcher Street, just three blocks from where I was constructing my new workspace on "A" Street in one of the many, mostly vacant, turn of the century factory buildings of an area on Boston's waterfront known as Fort Point. My blood was rising, my cheeks were hot and flushed. He'd be moving in within the next few days. His space was also not zoned as a legal live/workspace, but he'd be living there while the landlord looked the other way. His main concern was the structural integrity of the building since the floors in his studio had to carry a lot of weight. Life-sized figures in limestone and granite must be taken seriously. So far, I'd only seen the plaster relief he was working on when I walked in. My curiosity was piqued. I'd never known a stone carver before, and certainly not one who worked directly from life. He seemed like an anachronism. We were living in a time when abstract expressionism was dead, and minimalism was king. I had forced myself to try some minimalist drawings in grad school, and my effort seemed falsified, unnatural, far from my main love, drawing the human figure. It was the source of whatever power my artwork had - so regardless of the trends; I stuck with the figure. Evidently Robin had made the same decision. We were kindred spirits in that regard.

He suggested I meet him at his apartment later that evening and we could make a plan. He warned me that it was just a temporary crash pad that a friend was letting him use while she was out of town. The "she" part caught me off guard. Who is this "she" I wondered but didn't ask. I agreed to meet him there for a drink after work.

The rest of the day was experienced in a fog. I remember

entering the building on Newbury Street. The apartment number he gave me was two flights up. I was worried he wouldn't be there. I was also worried that he would be there.

I knocked.

The door opens immediately. It is him. The apartment is very dark, blinds drawn, sparsely furnished. I step gingerly inside. He has some candles burning on a fireplace mantle. Awkwardness. I've never felt so self-conscious. My body is getting in my way. He offers me a drink. Wine is sure to help the situation. He disappears and soon returns with two glasses and a bottle. He's prepared. That pleases me. I ask him about his history. He tells me he wasn't always an artist; he came to it later in life. He'd been in the Navy, done a tour of Vietnam. He's about 6 or 7 years older than me. His father had been a military man, but it wasn't a good fit for him, he bummed around after that, searching for something, he wasn't sure what. He did a few years in the forestry service, living alone in the woods for long periods of time. He also did a stretch working in the Lawrence Livermore Radiation Labs in California. He made many attempts to finish college and later, a graduate degree. Nothing clicked until he took a sculpture course. The physicality of stone carving, and I suspect the release of aggression that occurs in that act, was a perfect fit for him. He offered to show me photos. I was eager to see them.

He disappeared into the darkened hall and returned with two albums. We sat on the sofa together and page by page he showed me his life's work, complete from his days on a submarine when he was the quirky guy who painted figures, just cartoony things, on lockers and walls below decks. This was before he went to art school. The rest of the photos, mostly sculpture, were extraordinary. All the pieces were so beautiful, they could have occupied a Grecian building in ancient Athens. Female figures in various stages of dress or undress, but often gently carved clothing was a chance to hint seductively at the body underneath, besides revealing a spectacular skill at his craft.

I was excited. What a talent. I could not contain my enthusiasm. His arm had been resting along the top edge of the couch behind me. As his hand slid down embracing my shoulders, I raised my head and smiled. He pulled me towards him, his mouth was on my mouth. He was devouring me. I sensed myself being sucked up, enveloped, and absorbed by another being. We were suddenly standing. His searching hands were all over my body, touching everywhere at once. My skirt was at my hips. He backed me against a wall and then he was inside me. I felt electrocuted. I'd never had sex standing up. I was flying. I slowly descended. When I left for home later that evening, I knew my marriage was over.

Guilt was a new feeling for me, and I didn't like it. I snuck into the house that first night and Pete was already in bed. My 10-year-old daughter was asleep in her room. I showered and slinked into bed beside Pete. At that moment, I knew I had betrayed our marriage in a way that was irretrievable. Pete had accepted the fact I was moving into my studio at Fort Point to facilitate my work as an artist. It was a career move he thought was momentary insanity inspired by my "artsy-fartsy friends." He always thought I was too easily influenced. He believed it was temporary, and as soon as I regained my sanity I would move back home where I belong.

He had forgotten that I had displays of what some people might call, at the very least, mental instability, much earlier in our marriage. When Erika was about five years old, Pete and I were working together at the M.I.T. summer day camp. It was a program for children of faculty, kids from 6 to 14 (Erika got in because her dad was the director, and her mom ran the arts and crafts program.) That summer I began having what I could only call frequent out of body experiences. I did not do drugs, and I was not into any spirituality/guru or whatever sort of stuff. I would experience myself, my real self, from high up, looking down at me in my life going about my business, but the person on the ground wasn't me. The real me was the observer. It scared the shit out of me. One weekday I formally invited my husband to have lunch with me in the student center. This request was an unusual event because he and I had so many kids to deal with during the workday we never took time for lunch, let alone with each other in an adult arena. He absentmindedly agreed. We got our lunch trays in the student center cafeteria. I looked for a table where we could talk privately. I tried to tell him how afraid I was of this feeling, this sensation I was having, the fly on the wall looking down at myself. I cried. He listened to me. He cared about me, so I know he tried to understand. But he didn't.

"You'll be O.K. honey," he said. "You have paralysis of the analysis."

I felt lost, buried my panic, stirred the food on my plate, and was sorry I had revealed my anxiety.

With Robin, on that first night, pinned against the wall in his apartment, I neglected to tell him I was married. In my head, I was no longer married but tell that to the judge. The next day, a Saturday, I took Erika to work with me. The Gallery was between exhibitions, so the entire space was empty before the next bunch of artists came in to hang their paintings. I let Erika bring her new puppy, a black Peekapoo named Walter. I'd recently bought her this dog (she picked him out) as a kind of offering. I knew that soon her life would be shaken, I would be responsible for that, and I was trying to provide her with things that would help her deal with the emotional upheaval I knew was to come.

Renee and I were working on an application for an up-coming grant deadline. Erika was running around the gallery space like a little maniac with Walter yapping merrily along at her heels. She seemed ecstatic. So much space and no one yelling at her to be quiet. It soothed me to see her in this moment of innocent, childhood abandon.

Coming from the entryway, I heard the voice that made me melt. I looked up to see Robin sauntering in. He just "dropped by" to say hello. My jaw tightened; he saw the chaos of my kid and her dog running around the gallery. The child did not look anything like Renee, so who was left? The awkwardness of that moment still pains me. Erika sensed something was amiss and ran over to hug me.

Robin laughed, "So who is this?"

Erika looked shyly first at me, and then at him. I introduced them, "Robin is mommy's new friend."

A relentless desire to be with him propelled me through my days. At 14, I'd become sexually active and had had a wide range of experiences before I married Pete. Once I was married, I believed I was married and managed to be faithful and true and all that – whatever – but, like Jimmy Carter said, "I had lust in my heart."

Meeting Robin was like a nuclear explosion. Sexual experience on a whole new plane. After the chance encounter at the gallery with my child, I confessed that I was still married to her father and still living at home but with plans in the works to move out soon. Robin confessed that he had a long-term relationship with a woman he met in college, he never married and did not live with her, never planned to live with her, she'd had a hysterectomy so no children, and besides all that he was not sexually attracted to her. She smoked and smelled bad. Of course, I believed him!!! It didn't matter who he had or didn't have. If he was not a dad with kids - everything was up for grabs.

We found excuses to meet during the day. I had fantasies of walking along a downtown street with him and ducking into an alcove and unzipping his pants and holding his beautiful penis in my hands. A woman knows when a guy likes her. It's when she touches him, and he's ready, she looks at him, and he's ready. The other woman in his life did not seem to be a priority. I'd sneak out of my house to the pay phone on the corner to call him. He'd always be there. When it came to making plans to be together, I had the impression he accommodated me. So, while there was another woman, I never felt emotionally threatened.

There was plenty of risky behavior. It was 1980 and AIDS was still nowhere on the horizon. All the STDs were treatable. He and I never discussed it. We never used protection. I was still young enough to get pregnant, and if I did get pregnant, I would have had his baby. That's how potent the feeling was.

One night I was on my way to a gala event at the Institute of Contemporary Art. Being the token artist elected to serve on their Board of Directors provided access to the hoi polloi of the Boston art scene. A high-profile event for an emerging artist. It was very easy to take a short detour before I was due at the event to visit Robin at his studio on Melcher Street. He was pleased to see me. I wore a wine-colored silk dress, very delicate and floaty. Suffice it to say, we made good use of the time. The sex was spontaneous, mutually joyful and thrilling. At some point we had to stop, I was expected to be at this cultural event, on time. I put on my clothes, and Robin offered to walk me across the Summer Street Bridge to South Station where I had to catch the Red Line subway to Mass Ave. The velvety evening air enveloped us. As we walked, the warm, sticky ooze of his semen could not be ignored. I looked down at my silk dress as it blew between my legs and a huge dark stain started to form.

"Oh, my God, Robin, what can I do about this?" Suddenly I'd become Hester Prynne.

We were laughing, and he took my hand. We both dashed towards the lady's bathroom in South Station. No one else was there, luckily, so he came in with me. The dress was a two-piece affair, I easily slipped out of the skirt, and he helped rinse it in the sink. We tried drying it under the wall mounted hand dryer. It was getting later by the minute. I pulled the skirt back on and made a dash for the train, leaving him standing on the platform wearing a sheepish grin. By the time I got to the ICA, my clothes were almost dry. I walked in smiling. The Institute's director, Steven Prokopoff, greeted me with a glass of wine. I knew my paintings were under consideration for the next Boston Now exhibition. There was schmoozing to do as the evening stretched out ahead.

deep six

by Livio Farallo

i am waiting for change
as the bells of the abbey blow across centuries/
as smoke fills the nostrils/
as lake ontario rolls over and plays dead/

i am waiting to make a telephone call
with a dime that will never work
        and still not understanding how wires
                spank the sky/
                how any mountain will
                never fall down/
                        how snow rests in a
                        garbage can but melts on
                        the pavement.

and i am waiting at this truck stop
for you to phone me as we both
look for coins in hands that are gas tanks apart/
                and with eight cents left in my pocket
                and the sky singing everyone's name but yours
                i'm wondering, at last, how you
                can appear so incredibly beautiful
                and me, so incredibly far away/

Riverfront
by Sam Baldassari Jones

As children, we made games of the gallons: underwater worlds inhabited by two.

As teenagers, we tanned, splashed. Dared to jump from the highest rock.

As honeymooners, we waited for darkness, stripped, leapt: entangled in the current, each other's limbs.

As parents, we walked her patiently. Small steps, spying for fishies. Tiny hand touching water. *Cold.* You get used to it, we promised.

Grown now, she lives by the river. Walks us, patiently. Good for our joints, our lungs.

At night, we sneak away. Laughing like children, kissing like teens.

Submerged: even old limbs remember their way to underwater worlds.

Start Of Athletic-Artistic Romances

by Gerard Sarnat

For 7th time (so far)
in a half-century
Ger was spoiled
By pleasure
Getting to
Take boy/
Girlchick
To sports
Store to
Buy 1st
Mitt,
Bat.

This
Round
Helmets
Required
For T-ball
Otherwise
Same old
Rules apply:
Kid's love of
Equipment is
More important
Than perfect fit.

Flashing back to
My mid-1950's
When choosing
Your original
Slazenger's
Racquet to
Play tennis
Sarnat was
Smitten at
Sight by its
Rainbow
Colors.

Odd Socks and Sinks in Chaos

by Pat Dutt

The story appeared in the magazine's *Personal Experience* column. George always read the column's first paragraph, then picked out a middle paragraph, and finally read the last paragraph. If he wasn't too busy and there were enough potato chips left in the bag, he'd read the remaining inside paragraphs, in effect, reading the whole damn column.

The lover depicted in the narrative, Gerald (a gifted and creative individual) was kind of a jerk, and this gave George a tremendous feeling of superiority. Any piece of writing that could elicit a spontaneous smile was worth all the gold that his eccentric neighbor down the road had buried in his kale garden. Yet it seemed odd that both Gerald and George lived alongside a robust creek near a university. Odder still, they both taught the exact same third-year physics course. Their roofs leaked. Their sinks backed-up periodically. His socks never matched. Gerald was depicted as living in a whirlwind of confusion and chaos, and because he eschewed putting anything away there were electronics, most of it retired sound equipment, often in parts and pieces, scattered everywhere.

Only after George finished the column did he see the author's nom de plume.

"That's my house you described!" he told his girlfriend. Maggie and George had met three years ago at the *Native Plants Symposium* where Maggie had spoken about the birds and the bees. He held out the magazine to her so she could read the title, *Odd Socks and Sinks in Chaos*.

"How many people do you think live in houses with leaking roofs and plugged sinks?" Maggie said. "Probably half of New York State."

"But the column says *Personal Experience*. That means non-fiction. And if anyone who reads this knows you, then they will assume that this is about *me*."

"I think we can agree that such writing is often a mix of fiction and fact."

"In this instance, Maggie, I don't agree at all."

"George, you *don't* understand," Maggie said, gently putting her right hand above her chest. "Writing comes from the heart. A writer needs those intriguing details to keep a story moving, especially given a person's limited attention span. Or the reader gives up. Why write if the reader's going to give up?"

He stood there, shocked, trying not to feel aggrieved.

"George, you're my muse!"

"But it says '*He* insists on wearing non-matching socks.' I've never insisted on any such thing. And where did this come from, 'He enjoys dining in the nude and he doesn't care if the neighbors peek through the forsythia hedge and see his manhood'? You make him sound like a pervert."

"If you let your conscious mind run the show then the protagonist has zero dimension. No mystery. Anyway, a hint of sex is good because sex is drama, and drama engages." Maggie smiled, and raised her left eyebrow seductively.

"At my expense," he said.

"At your self-affirmation. Maybe you'll even think differently about yourself."

He did not see that at all. Maybe he had to sit with the idea for a while.

It was May, nearly dusk, so the evening symphony of bird whistles and cooing had commenced. Glancing out of the kitchen window to the forest lining the creek, George saw a Downy woodpecker rhythmically hitting on an ash tree. As a physicist, when he heard such pleasing melodies, he imagined sound waves building and refracting as they moved at approximately 1,087 feet per-second through air. Blue Jays flew from one spruce tree to another, yakking the whole time and looking down on the world with amusement. The shallow pond beside the creek, a premier hangout for peepers, rocked nightly.

"I write because I care, and I care about you, and you're on my mind! That's a compliment. Yes?"

"How would you feel if I wrote about you?"

"Not a concern."

"You're sure?" He narrowed his eyes, and held the bag of chips out to her. She took one.

"Be my guest." She sat down on a stool, folded her hands, and smiled up at him.

"Julia gets up every morning at four to work. She's always working. At her job or writing. Obsessively and organically. She's a maniac. Then she leaves dishes in the sink and doesn't wash a single dish until the cupboard is bare, or the ants have moved on."

"Wait a minute – ants? Everyone gets ants now and then."

"*Odd Socks and Sinks in Chaos*?"

"Okay fine."

"As a biologist and responsible citizen, she's deep into horticulture and sustainability, so she pees in a bucket, claiming the nitrates, if diluted, are the ideal plant fertilizer."

Maggie stared hard at George. "What else would it be, George? You make me sound like some kind of weirdo!"

"This not necessarily about you, Maggie. Writing is a mixture of fact and fiction? I'm not finished. She likes to go on long, walks pointing out moss and lichens, all the while quietly imitating bird calls. She knows 150. Her companion can barely get a word in edgewise." He made sure she was looking at him when he added, "And she's nearly 60 years old."

"Must you mention my age?"

George grinned at her in his particularly devilish way and she knew what was coming.

"If you want to sell it," Maggie said, giving him the same look back, "you have to add some one-on-one."

"You mean sex."

"The horizontal bop. Right now."

So George put *Bachman Tuner Overdrive* on the stereo, and Maggie got the cold beer. They went into the bedroom and plugged in the string of lights that framed the windows facing the woods. As *You Ain't Seen Nothing Yet* played, George made a stab at the meaning of bird calls, and this provoked fits of ridiculous, snorting laughter, putting them both in the mood to finally, get down to business.

Dancing

by Renee Williams

Uneven planks, calloused wood weathered by nor'easters
lead over the Atlantic, sand sharks below graze for chum
the bar at the end of the pier is a centerpiece for Budweiser and
Hank Williams
while cloggers shimmy to "Mustang Sally" for the third time of
the evening.

Those who fish huddle near the benches at the edge of the deck
their Lowe's buckets filled with mullet for bait or the catch of
the night
knives at the ready sit on the fencing
the strawberry moon blesses all beneath her.

The bartender tells us the storm coming into the Gulf bears
watching
you never when those tropical depressions will build up steam
chiming into our waters
reminding us of Hurricane Hugo that decimated this pier not
so long ago.

A pelican loiters nearby, waiting for remnants left behind
this one is not as fast as the grackles or gulls
occasionally a child will toss a small blue fish its way.

Eric Clapton's vocals cloud the evening air
"Wonderful Tonight" causes the cloggers to take a rest
and slowly couples set their Yuengling bottles on the tables
sticky from stale ketchup spills and maple syrup from the
breakfast fare.

You take my hand and lead me to the dance floor
the salty wind whips my hair into my face
you push it aside with your hands
and gazing into your eyes,
the world stops.

Best Foot Forward

by Nam Hoang Tran

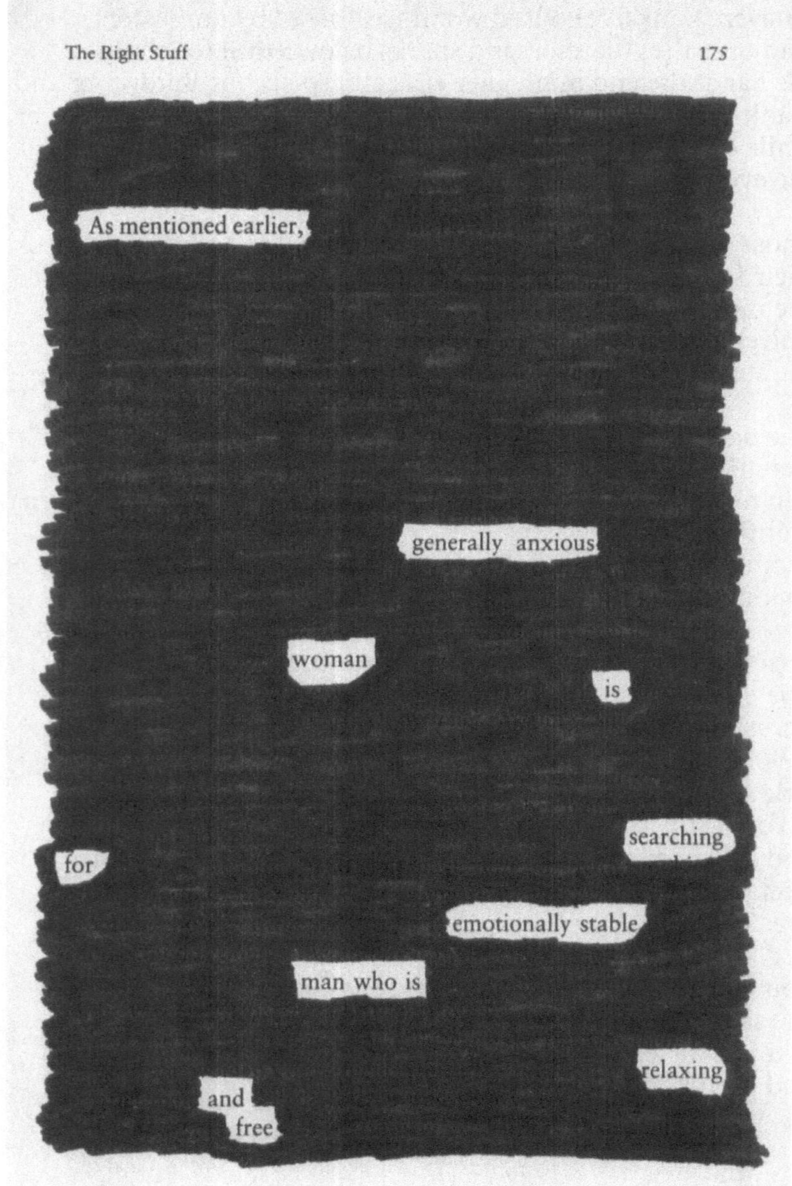

Arch of Aorta
by Junix Seraphim

To kiss open

Don't mind me, swallowing

Bowl of your mouth

Nerve bundle berries

of your throat

I can barely make out the purples

Small intestine

alluding to arching my spine

of blackberry vine

When you said I was brave

Burst Bloomed from my mouth

I want to Bury Plant Dive

Your airways stuffed

Pressed against the pith of you

Your heart is a beating thing

Your lungs Life was

Real only for the moment

In the valves

Do you even know

your mouth

Teeth from the shallow

Tonguing for

Coiled tangles

Inside of you is so dark

of your pink

I'm sorry I can't say I love you unless

Mimicry of bend

It's just that

Several golden stamens

Shrapnel from my orifice

All of my tongues inside you

with my flesh anther and filament

At the aortic root of it all

Tucked behind and between

the greatest liminal space of all

I was as close to you as your blood

Of your aortic arch

your aorta is

time the roots

the entire time Look
            I'm pulling
                  them up
All your red string

in my fingers

How fucking long

The roots were inside the whole

were on the inside

from inside you

cat cradle

Pay Attention
by Peggy Heitmann

I ask my husband,
Did you notice the new
apartments downtown?
He looks at me curiously before he answers.

I amaze my husband
by my lack of observation.
I fail to note
road construction,
high-rise offices,
those apartments built 5 years ago,
and highway detour signs.

I cocoon myself in a small world.
I'm attracted to only important details:
the enchanting cadence of his voice,
the rise and fall of his chest when he breathes,
the smell of his cologne,
the feel of his hand as he brushes my cheek,
the way his eyes soften when he smiles at me.

Beauty and the Beast
by Justin Ratcliff

Show me your wrenched out heart
I want to hold it in my clingy claws
I want to bite down on the fleshy fibers
As the blood drips down my gullet

Give me your innocent eyes
I want to see what the esse entails
Slurping down the milky mess
Savoring all your scene things

My love for you is terribly taboo
My hunger for you is carelessly cannibalistic
My attraction for you animalistic and alien
My desire for you borders on illicit insanity

good night
by Francesca J. Sidoti

some sleep carries dreams
to a far heaven
I watch them roll
beneath your eyes sands
perched in dunes, trailing
broken chimes.

the flower moon sees
you in your bed
on a forest floor
where moss makes bark
soft. Arms folded, you
catch leaves from the
blanket wind.

sleep finds you without
dreams your face turned
to the trees still standing
some nights sea and
mountains come when trains
bring them rumbling it
is still enough to hear.
still flowing asleep you
welcome them.

violet air drifts, stars
lift themselves to see
you tucked in tumbled
leaves. hours are solemn.
you smile for them,
Waking much later in
the light.

Harvey Wallbanger and a

by Nicholas Yandell

I hate myself for showing up to work. What a waste. I've danced four sets for worse than no one, just those who return my failing attempts at sensuality with a dehumanizing stare. I'm continually reminding myself that it's not my fault that I'm not making money. Not helping though. Neither are all the drinks I've had. Now it's the bottom of the barrel, the club is empty, and I've still got another hour to go.

I don't even give a shit what I put on at this point. Some gray briefs will do. Don't bother with the jewelry. A red baseball cap so I don't have to fix my hair. Who the fuck am I trying to appeal to anyway?

Slamming my locker shut, I can't even remotely get into a good headspace. As I'm leaving our prep area, I'm passing the bar, and a guy I've never seen before walks through the door. Holding a nearly-finished drink, with just a few ice cubes and a little stir straw, he sits down at a table near the door. Silver-haired, dressed formally in a suit and tie, he's definitely the type one would call a "gentleman." I'm immediately thinking: *I'm not gonna be his type and I don't have it in me to get rejected again.* I should just go sit in the locker space, lay low, and wait out the night. Fuck it though. I got one more try left, then I'll throw in the towel.

Adjusting my cap, squeezing out that last bit of remaining willpower, I swagger up to the gentleman's table. As I put my arm around him, I say:

"Welcome to your own private den of sin! Anything I can do to make your stay more pleasing?"

"Oh. Um. No. I'm quite okay. But thanks for offering, mate."

Mate? I like that. And he's got a strong thick accent. I'm immediately thinking: *Okay, now there's potential here.* I continue with:

"Anytime! So, I take it you're visiting. Where are you from?"

"Yeah, that's right. Last day of my trip. I'm here from Sydney, Australia."

"Nice. I figured you were from somewhere down under. Thrilled you stopped in to see us! What's your name anyway?"

"I'm Lachlan."

"Lachlan? Never heard that name in my life. It's pretty cool."

"Well, thank you, and what's your name, mate?"

"I'm Holden."

"Holden? Ah, yes. Like Holden Caulfield."

"Very good! Yeah, I'm basically him, only now he's a faggot, who's all grown up, and stripping for a living. Yep, that pretty much sums me up."

He looks a little shocked by what I've said and I realize that not everyone's so accustomed to my casual use of that word.

"Sorry, if my language is a little harsh. I didn't mean to offend a kind sir like you."

He immediately smiles, then laughs, before saying:

"Well Holden, I think you're actually a lot nicer than you want people to think you are."

"Uh… thanks. I guess. That's a very strange compliment, but I'll take it."

"Is it a compliment, or just an observance?"

"I don't know, Lachlan. Good question. Hmm. Well, how

about this one: I think I like you a whole lot more than I expected I would."

"I'd say that's a compliment, but it might not be much of one. Your expectations of me might've been really low. Maybe you assumed I was just a lecherous old man looking to take advantage of a young chap like you."

"Oh, I'm not worried about that. No one takes advantage of me anymore. I've been burned too many times. Now I'm just a cynical fuck, who's always on his guard."

"I have no doubt you can take care of yourself, and you clearly know how to hold your own against a tipsy old traveler like me, but I doubt you're as cynical as you say you are. I bet you're actually a romantic at heart; you just don't know it yet."

"Yeah, okay. You're really grasping at straws with that statement."

"That's quite true. I really am."

I look down and his finger is holding the stirring straw in his empty glass. I shake my head, chuckle, and say:

"Okay. Yeah. Real clever. Bravo, good sir."

"Glad I could make you laugh! Also, looks like I'm in dire need of another drink. Can I interest you in something, Holden?"

"You know what Lachlan? Sure. Why not?"

Following him to the bar, he says to Anthony, the bartender:

"You know how to make a Harvey Wallbanger, mate?"

I've never heard of the drink, and apparently neither has Anthony, but Lachlan quickly tells him how to make it and then adds: "And whatever this chap would like as well."

"I'll take a Slippery Nipple," I say, looking directly at Lachlan. He's amused and responds with:

"That's quite the name. Where did you first encounter a drink like that?"

"Oh, there was this guy I used to date, a bartender, and he used to give me this shot. I still enjoy people's reactions when I order it."

"Do you think of him when you drink it?"

"I mean, maybe. A little."

"Nothing like a little alcohol to bring out the sweet reminiscence of a former flame, right? Sounds wistfully romantic for such a cynic as yourself."

"Please. I wouldn't call him a flame, whatever that means. We just fucked few dozen times over a couple months. There was no romance there. That's never been something I've had any interest in, at all."

"And yet, when you have this drink, he comes to mind. He must have had some impact on you. Do you miss him?"

"I mean, I guess. It didn't end badly between us or anything. Breaking up was just the practical thing to do. He moved across the ocean; there was no point in keeping a long-distance thing going. Enough about me though. Tell me about your weird-ass drink?"

"Well, I didn't used to care for this drink at all, but I've had enough of them on this trip that it's starting to grow on me."

"Okay, so now I'm curious. Why would you drink a whole lot of drinks that you never liked in the first place?"

"It's my husband's favorite drink."

"Yeah, okay, well, still doesn't make sense. If it's not your thing, just let him drink it! It's not like you need to have the same tastes as your husband. Couples are so fucking weird."

"I won't argue with you there. I just like to drink it because it makes me think of him."

"So... What? Is he at home or something and you're home-sick?"

"Not exactly, mate. He passed away two months ago."

"Ah, okay... Listen: I could tell you I'm sorry, and feel really bad about him passing, and make this awkward, but I'm not going to do that, because I don't think that's what you want."

"Hmm. A bold choice. You're definitely perceptive, Holden. I think you're also quite good at your job."

"Yeah, well, a lot of people get really shy around us dancers, so we have to figure out what they want whether they'll tell us or not. Let me say this though, Lachlan: I admire you for not just lying around at home, mourning, and getting all caught up in that sentimental bullshit. You're out living your life and seeing the world!"

"Well, I won't lie to you. This whole trip wasn't my idea. It was my husband, Aiden's. He always loved the American West Coast, ever since he lived here as a young surfer lad. We'd planned this trip for a couple of years, but never got to go together of course. It was actually supposed to be our honeymoon. How's that for being sentimental?"

"Wow. How long were you two married?"

"Only 1 year, 2 months, and 16 days. We were together for 51 years though. Got married on the 50th anniversary of the day we met. I bet you're really judging me now, aren't you, Mister Cynic?"

"Only a little bit. But honestly, I'm also confused. For guys like you two, why'd you wait so long to get married?"

"Well, it was only legal less than a decade ago, and by that time, we debated whether it even mattered for us at that point. In the end, when he got sick, it became important to us for many reasons."

"I get it. I think at that point it goes way beyond anything sentimental and I'm glad you got to have that."

"Doesn't appeal to you though, does it, mate? The idea of spending your life with another person in a 'romantic' way?"

"Well Lachlan, since you're such an expert on the subject, tell me, what does it even mean to be in a romantic relationship? What makes it different than any other relationship?"

"To me, it's less about what romance is and really more about what it does to its participants. Through the intimate ways in which you know another person and they know you. How you open up to each other, with such vulnerability, that your time spent together seems to alter both of your chemical existences. What do you think of that?"

"It can't be easy to open up like that."

"No, it isn't, but once you've been there with someone, it becomes a necessity and after such an experience, it's awfully hard to even remember what your former life was like."

"Honestly, that's never happened to me and I don't think it ever will. I wouldn't even know how to start being that vulnerable."

"You do exactly what you're doing right now. Even just admitting that lack of experience is opening up, revealing yourself, and being more vulnerable."

"What if this is all fake though and I'm just lying to you? Then I'm not really opening up, am I?"

"But you're not lying to me, Holden, are you?"

"I don't even know what's true anymore, Lachlan. I feel like I've lived so many different lies over the years. Here, as a dancer, and in life in general. I lie about my age, I tell people I'm 27, but I'm actually 36. Even the name I told you, Holden, that's not my real name, that's just who I dance as."

"I think you're a whole lot better at this vulnerability thing than you think. Just look at how much you divulge when you let your guard down for a moment."

"Okay, good sir. You were sly and got that out of me, but slow down. This has got to go both ways. What about you? It's two months after losing your husband of fifty-some years, and here you are, on a different continent, on the last day of your trip, drinking with some stripper in a club at 1:30 AM. What're you even doing here? You can't tell me you're not running away from something."

He doesn't respond, and after a minute or so, I lick the last drops out of my shot glass and add:

"I'm sorry if I went too far with that."

"No, Holden. You're right. I am running away. It's hard facing every day with the same longing to wake up next to him, and maybe that's why I left. I hoped that I could fool myself into thinking, for a time, that I was just away, and I'd eventually be home and he'd be waiting for me there. Now it's just so painful imagining anything after this trip, a trip that meant so much to him. That's why I'm here in this club. Being adventuresome, doing what he would have done and going where he would have gone. Still offering him my love as best as I know how. Til death do us part and as long as I can stretch it beyond. But when I get to the tips of all these loose ends, I don't know what I'll hold onto, and that's what scares me the most."

I have no idea what I can possibly say after this. This night has become way too much for me to handle and I'm not comfortable with any of it. Just as I'm making plans to get hell out of this conversation, he smiles and says:

"Another slippery nipple for you, mate?" He then laughs, and adds: "That is a fun name to say. SliP-Purry NiP-Pull! Might have to try one of those. Please, join me for one more drink?"

Fuck it. I smile back at him and say: "It would be my pleasure, good sir. Only this time, I gotta try one of those Harvey

Wallbangers!"

"Anthony, another Harvey Wallbanger and a Slippery Nipple, only this time we're switching places."

"Switching places? You know, I can't even imagine what that would be like!"

"The young cynic switching with the old sentimental sap. A whole new spin on the Prince and the Pauper, right?"

I laugh, but I'm not feeling that great all of a sudden. Lachlan immediately notices and says:

"What's wrong, mate?"

"I'm gonna be honest with you, Lachlan. Sometimes it does bother me that I can't even begin to picture myself having something like what you and Aiden had. I didn't choose to be like this. It's sad to think that maybe I could have actually had "emotional availability" or whatever guys I've dated have always said I'm lacking. I just didn't grow up with anyone who cared about me. Everyone let me down and left me behind. And when I was all alone as a little kid, I knew I just had myself to rely on and that was it and I don't think I've ever been able to see beyond that. Pretty fucking sad, right?!"

He puts his hand on my shoulder and I immediately feel embarrassed, switch up my thoughts, and nervously chuckle as I say:

"Dammit. I'm sorry. I'm just really feeling all the drinks I've had. I'm sure you wanted an escape tonight, not to listen to some stripper babble on about his difficult childhood."

"No, you're wrong, Holden. Nothing could make me happier than to hear you open up like that. Makes me feel like there's a reason to still be alive."

Before I can reply to what he's saying, they're calling "Holden" on the speaker. For a moment, I had forgotten where I was and even what I did for a living. I say to him:

"Dammit. Hold my drink, will you please? I gotta go move my body for 10 minutes."

Right before I head to the stage, I get a sudden idea and stop by the DJ real quick. Right as I get on stage, the song starts: *All the Lovers* by Kylie Minogue. Moving my body and mouthing the words, I direct them right at Lachlan. He shakes his head, laughs, and walks over to the edge of the dance floor saying:

"I know this one! Aiden was a big fan."

"I kinda hoped you would. She was honestly the only Australian singer I could think of in the moment, but I'm happy it worked out."

"It's perfect, mate. You know how to really make my night."

As he's watching my performance, I get another idea. Walking off the stage, grabbing his hand, I say: "Here, dance with me, good sir."

Without a word, he takes my hand, spins me around, and even dips me. Not my style of dancing, but damn, he's a good partner.

For the rest of my set, we chat, I do my thing, and he playfully slips me some bills so, as he says, he can have the "full Holden experience." When the bartender calls me off stage, and we head back to the table with our drinks, I pick up my Harvey Wallbanger, and as I'm sipping it, he suddenly stares at me and says:

"Maybe it's just this lighting, but seeing you there, dressed how you are, holding that drink, you look just like Aiden when I first met him at that beach bar. Even your rougher speech immediately brought him to mind, but I'm probably just seeing him everywhere right now. Sorry, Holden. We both know I'm just an old, sentimental fool."

"I mean you're definitely sentimental as fuck, but you're no fool, Lachlan. By the way, my real name's Chance. Not that you asked, but tonight, since I've already been spilling my guts way more than I ever planned, why not? Hmm. And if you don't mind me asking, what did Aiden used to call you?"

"Oh, well he always called me Lanny."

"Great. You willing to try something with me, real quick?"

He shrugs, then nods, and I add: "Let me try being him for a moment. How does that sound, Lanny?"

"Anything for you, Aiden." He starts tearing up immediately as he says the name.

"Lanny, you don't have to worry about honoring me anymore. You made me happy for more than five decades, you offered me so much love, more than most people can even imagine in multiple lifetimes, and I know you'll never forget about me. But what I do need from you, is to take all that love, which right now seems to have no place to go, and keep sharing it with others for the rest of your days. Maybe there's some damn lucky bloke out there, who'll be fortunate enough to be a new chapter in your life, and if he'll make you happy, don't you hesitate. But if not, you do what you're clearly so good at doing and take that kind of love and share it with others, especially those who may never have otherwise believed it could exist. Hell, maybe even find a cynical fuck, who works at a strip club, but now can't stop tearing up even as he's saying all this; wishing so bad that he could be like Aiden and have someone like you in his life."

He takes my hand and I immediately bury my face into his shoulder and I'm actually crying. Me? Fucking losing it, right here. He seems surprised, but just holds me for a second. Then says:

"Chance. What an appropriate name for someone like you at the place you are in your life. Such a reminder that you have everything you need to find that love, if you'll just give it a chance. But something's been lit in you tonight and I don't believe it's ever gonna die away. It might take some time for you to adjust, and no one ever gets really great at being vulnerable, but it definitely gets easier."

"I'll take your word on that. I know you wouldn't lie to me."

At that moment, Anthony announces last call, and Lachlan says:

"I guess that means we should be on our ways. Hope you've got something warm to change into."

"Thanks to that last drink, and meeting you, I'm feeling pretty warm inside right now. Confused as fuck, but warm all the same."

"Good on you, mate. I knew you had a warm soul, it just needed to be thawed out a bit."

With that, he reaches into his pocket and hands me his card. Then adds:

"I don't know when or if I'll ever be back this way, but you can always reach out to me anytime you'd like. And if you ever decide to visit down under, there's always a roof over your head."

He extends his hand out to shake mine, but I pull him in for a long hug instead. When we release, we just smile at each other and I say:

"Alright, alright. Don't make me cry again, asshole. Seriously, you get home safe, and for fuck's sake, find someone to give all that love to. Bye Lanny."

He pauses for a second and looks a little wistful, so I add:

"It's okay, you can call me Aiden one more time if you want. I'll never have a problem hearing the epic amount of love you put into those two little syllables as they roll off your tongue."

"No. It's okay. I don't need to say his name to direct that kind of love and I don't need two syllables to do it. So let's you and I end this night with some beginnings. Me with the start of something new to live for, and you with the first of many times you'll hear such an immense love packed into that one syllable that represents who you are. You ready for it, mate?"

"I am, good sir."

"Great. Well then, you take care, *Chance*."

Metric Apology

by Anna Laura Falvey

Long-haired Apollo sits with legs splayed out
in perspective slant, upright bass in hand, plucking
steady, mooded, sweat beading his pulsed temple,
beating in dissonant tones that wrap deftly over,

around his triple knotted fingers, doting on the
wide frequency which sounds through the black
as one would on the brow of a lover. He has
just lost his girl, and so he lilts, jaw cutting sound

into resounding patterns of the whole: whole;
half; quarter; eighth; sixteenth; thirty-second;
sixty-fourth; one twenty-eighth… and on he goes,
pulling time so thin and sound so distant that

there opened a new tilt in the night sky, like
a sloe eye, into which if one stepped, would find
that glass could be blown from the wind
and the birds always look black and clear

and slow against a perpetual orange. And through
this tilt a sister, Artemis, rubbing her strong jaw,
the same as his, stepped, and placed a cooling hand
on his shoulder. She sang low and calm, steady

and strong, and he heard her from the tips
of his hair to the strings of his upright bass.
As she sang, his notes grew longer, vowel
sounds beginning to reappear in place of

the staccato shrieks of false love. As she
sang, the lines of the harmony fell together
like the closing of a drawbridge at day's end
and the two sang, in cadence old and immutable.

Is this a fucking love poem?
by Timothy Arliss OBrien

This isn't a love poem. It's something else entirely.
This isn't a love poem: it's a sunny afternoon with us airing our
grief in the city park.

This isn't a love poem. It's that time you couldn't stop staring at
me rain soaked after we ran to the car, and the way your soft
lips found their path to my forehead.

This isn't a love poem - it's just me. It's always been me.

This isn't a love poem, this is how I wish things were,
 with us spilling it everywhere,
words on a page.

This isn't a love poem: I dare you, try to tell me it is.
Break my heart and leave me worse for wear.
Make this year one I will cry about for a decade in every dark
dive bar in this city.

This isn't a love poem no matter how much we scream at each
other. It never will be.

This isn't a love poem and I'm not in love.

And I'm not entirely sure I am capable.

This isn't a love poem and I am not ok with this.
I have labored too long and beat myself up
Over the pain and mistreatment
That my soul has endured in this life.
Please,
Don't tell me this is a love poem
that is leading me
to be trapped in that cycle.

This isn't a love poem. It's just my heart ripping out of my chest,
        and dissolving into words on a page.

This isn't a love poem: this is my white flag.
        Soaked in blood and sweat saying, "I… cannot… do this…
                anymore."

This isn't a love poem. It's a stillness.
A quiet moment right after the beginning raindrops.
A hushed whisper across a crowded cafe, "I'm glad I found you."
A lost memory.
Maybe the time they got our order wrong
and we vowed to never go there again,
Lest we separate over it.

This isn't a love poem. It's a peace treaty with an "et tu brute?" a
few seconds later.

This isn't a love poem: This is me lying under oath:
This is a fucking love poem.

Countless

by Kathryn Paulsen

Isn't it strange the way you're always saying
something I'd thought just the other hour or day
or the other way around? Or maybe,
each was thinking the same phrase at the same second,
just a question of who trots it out first:
makes the other laugh or sigh, inside or out.
That day you admired an ear lobe in the sun,
same day, indoors, I was writing of the light on yours,
rendering it transparent, trapping the fly of my eye
in your red web.

Repetition, you said one night at dinner,
is what interests me about love affairs
that go on longer than two months. By then,
you've told all the stories, you begin
to hear them again.
                      An hour before,
alone, I'd mused: *Look at the repetition.*
Hear what he tells you again and again,
what you don't want to—let it sink in.

Dreams—if you remembered more,
I'd be dreaming yours, or you mine. Alike
(we quibble, not quarrel). Different:
I won't count the ways.
You don't need me to say
something else nibbles at you than
nibbles at me.

A Winter's Night
by Lynette Esposito

I look up
to feel
the flickers of light
burning
with silver- blue flames
just out of reach.

The tips of my fingers almost touch
the fire
as
I stretch high and far
to where I believe
you have gone.

I am breathless
from the frosted air
on a winter's night
in the country
where stars are aplenty
but I am alone.

Epilogue
by Alixa Writes

All my life, I waited for love
like pineapple. Sopping bites,
hair bristling on skin, tangy
and biting. I waited for

the nibble on my tongue.
It never came. You came,
and you were oxygen.

You were misting rain,
not tidal waves. All my life,
I watched my father hail,
and I bent towards blue.

How to know love,
it isn't biting. Some days,
it smacks of nothing.

You scrub the petals
from my skin. You wipe
the juice pooling beneath
my chin. All my life,

I followed flames. Now
here you are, and
nothing aches.

BIOS

NIDHI AGRAWAL

Nidhi's writings have been featured by *Quadrant Australia*, *Girl Talk HQ*, *eShe Magazine*, University of California, *Riverside*, *Say it Forward*, Chicago School of Arts, Lewis Clark State College's literary journal, St. Francisco University's journal, *The Elevation review* (Kneeland Poetry Inc.), *The Dillydoun Review*, *Xavier Review Press*, California State Poetry Society, *Signal Mountain Review*- The University of Tennessee, *Chronogram Magazine*, *Letters* (Yale University), *Setu Journal*, *Spill Word Press South Asian Today*, *Indian Periodical*, *Rising Phoenix Review*, Life in 10 minutes press, *Ariel Chart*, *Women's Web*, *Women for One*, *Lekh*, *Garland Magazine*, and *Muse India*. She is the author of "Confluence".

VALERIE ANNE BURNS

Valerie Anne Burns has had essays from her book, *Caution: Mermaid Crossing, Voyages of a Motherless Daughter* published in Sea to Sky Review, The Remnant Archive, Libretto Magazine and HerStry. Essays in print include *Chicken Soup for the Soul: Tough Times Won't Last but Tough People Will* and *Rituals* Anthology by Bell Press. Additionally, she's had a poem published in *Writing Through the Apocalypse* by Weeping Willow Press. In September 2021, she received a Finalist Award from Page Turner Awards in the category of manuscript submission and was awarded scholarships to the 2019 Santa Barbara Writers Conference and the 2016 Prague Summer Writing Program. In addition, she was sponsored on a trip to Italy and The Dominican Republic for a breast cancer survivor retreat, where an essay from her book became a launching point for the workshop she created and presented, "Living and Healing Through Color." She traveled to Rome September 2022 for the same nonprofit where she blogged about her experience. She previously worked in Hollywood as a story editor and in production, as well as, having her own business as a makeover specialist for home décor and wardrobe. Santa Barbara is home, and the place where Valerie Anne has survived breast cancer. Being near the ocean brings out her "inner mermaid" and gives her the peace and clarity she needs to write, along with the strength and grace she needs to mother herself through the stormiest weather.

CYNTHIA CLOSE

Armed with an MFA from Boston University Cynthia plowed her way through several productive careers in the arts including instructor in drawing and painting, Dean of Admissions at The Art Institute of Boston,

founder of ARTWORKS Consulting, and president of Documentary
Educational Resources - a nonprofit film distribution company. She now
claims to be a writer.

MICKEY COLLINS
Mickey ~~rights wrongs~~. Mickey ~~wrongs rites~~. Mickey writes words, sometimes
wrong words but he tries to get it write.

SARAH DENISON
Sarah Denison is an English language teacher from Kentucky. Many years
ago, she worked as an editor and writer for her university's newspaper and
literary journals. She enjoys memoirs, literary fiction, poetry, mysteries,
science nonfiction, and cozy sci-fi. Her favorite place to read is in a tent by
flashlight.

DAVID DE YOUNG
David de Young recently completed an MFA with NYU's low residency
creative writing program in Paris. He's the proprietor of a small independent
publisher, Nordic Moon Press. He lives in Finland with his wife and three
children.

DESIREE DUCHARME
Desiree Ducharme is a writer. The greatest romance of my life has been with
used books. Mystery? Check. Excitement? Check. Remoteness from
everyday life? Check. Associated with love? Absolutely. It's more than a
passing fancy. Def not a fad. This is more than a "phase" or adolescent
obsession. It might be an unhealthy addiction. If it is, I'm not looking for a
cure. You can read more at desireeducharme.com

PAT DUTT
Pat Dutt's short stories and flash fictions have been published in *The
Louisville Review, Emrys Journal, Caustic Frolic, America Writers Review*, and
other literary magazines. She is the author of the non-fiction book, *The Good
Moms, Their Children, and Friendship*. Her home is in central New York
where she taught high school science and worked for many years as a
landscape estimator. She also volunteers for a mental health organization,
and writes a blog (mentalchill.org) along with her son, Ben.

LYNETTE G. ESPOSITO
Lynette G. Esposito, MA Rutgers, has been published in *Poetry Quarterly,
North of Oxford, Twin Decades, Remembered Arts, Reader's Digest, US1*, and
others. She was married to Attilio Esposito and lives with eight rescued
muses in Southern New Jersey.

Robert Eversmann
Robert Eversmann works for *Deep Overstock*.

Anna Laura Falvey
Anna Laura Falvey (she/her) is a Brooklyn-based poet and theater-maker.
She is a graduate of Bard College with degrees in Classics & Written Arts,
with a specialty in Ancient Greek tragedy and poetry, where she spent her
college career blissfully hidden behind the Circulation and Reference desks
at the Stevenson Library, where she worked. Anna Laura is currently serving
as an ArtistYear Resident Teaching Artist and Senior Fellow, teaching Poetry
in Queens, NY. Her written work is forthcoming with Querencia Press, &
Bloodletter Magazine, and has appeared in *Ev0ke Magazine*, *Club Plum*,
Caustic Frolic, *Ouch! Collective*, multiple issues of *Deep Overstock*, *Icarus
Magazine*, and has been featured on the Deep Overstock podcast.

Livio Farallo
Livio Farallo is co-founder and co-editor of Slipstream, currently in its 43rd
year of operation, publishing general poetry and art works, single-author
works, and themed poetry and art works. He is Professor of Biology at
Niagara County Community College in Sanborn, New York and his work
has appeared or is forthcoming, in *North Dakota Quarterly*, *Cordite Review*,
Triggerfish, *Panoplyzine*, *Adelaide Lit. Mag.*, *J Journal*, and elsewhere.

Lorenzo Fusini
Lorenzo Fusini is a proofreader, copyeditor, swimming instructor, and data
scientist with a PhD in Engineering Cybernetics. He's an Entry-Level
Member of the Chartered Institute of Editing and Proofreading and abides
by its Code of Practice. He enjoys any activity that enriches his mind and
expands his knowledge, or simply makes him laugh out loud. His other
passions are reading (especially science fiction and weird fiction), cultural
awareness, board/video/role-playing games, freediving, sports (mostly
rugby, tennis, and volleyball), food, and hanging out with friends. He lives in
Norway with his wife and two children. His LinkedIn profile is
www.linkedin.com/in/lorenzo-fusini.

Helga Gruendler-Schierloh
Helga Gruendler-Schierloh is a bilingual writer with a degree in journalism
and graduate credits in linguistics. Her articles, essays, short stories, and
poetry have appeared in the USA, the UK, Canada, and South Africa. Her
debut novel, *Burying Leo, a Me Too story*, won second place in women's
fiction during Pen Craft Awards' 2018 writing contest.

Heather Hambley
Heather is a Latin teacher turned translator. She has a BA in Classics from Reed College, where she developed a deep passion for Latin poetry and mythological women, especially Helen of Troy. She currently lives in Central Oregon with her husband Andy and their 15yo doggo Mo. She loves horror movies, particularly anything cozy or campy. Her dream is to translate Latin in the horror space, so hit her up with your spells, spooks, and spoofs. Heather's website is latinklub.wordpress.com.

Peggy Heitmann
Peggy Heitmann has published poems and forthcoming in *Remington Review*, *Months to Years*, *Last Leaves*, and *The Impostor*, among others. She considers herself both word & visual artist, and a medium. Peggy lives in Raleigh, NC area with her husband and two cats.

Paul Hostovsky
Paul Hostovsky's poems appear and disappear simultaneously (Voila!) and have recently been sighted in places where they pay you for your trouble with your own trouble doubled, and other people's troubles thrown in, which never seem to him as great as his troubles, though he tries not to compare. Website: paulhostovsky.com

RJ Equality Ingram
RJ Equality Ingram is a poet from Vermilion, Ohio who lives in Portland, Oregon & works as a bookseller for Goodwill Industries of the Columbia Willamette. RJ Received his MFA in creative writing with concentrations in poetry & creative nonfiction from Saint Mary's College of California & has work published in *White Stag*, *Pinwheel Journal*, *Alice Blue Review*, *Dreginald* as well as others. RJ's cat Brenda lost a leg in an RSVP to the prince's ball. Follow @RJEquality

Sam Baldassari Jones
My work has appeared in *Eunoia Review*, *100-Word Story*, *Flash Fiction Magazine*, and *NYCMidnight*, where my micro-fiction story was selected third among seven thousand writers. I received my MFA from Brooklyn College in 2018.

BEE LB
BEE LB is an array of letters, bound to impulse; a writer creating delicate connections. they have called any number of places home; currently, a single yellow wall in Michigan. they have been published in *FOLIO*, *Roanoke Review*, and *Figure 1*, among others. they are a poetry reader for Capsule Stories. their portfolio can be found at twinbrights.carrd.co

Timothy Arliss Obrien
Timothy Arliss OBrien (he/they) is an interdisciplinary artist in music composition, writing, and visual art. He has premiered a range of music from opera to film scores to electronic ambient projects. He has published several books of poetry, (*The Queer Revolt, Dear God I'm a Faggot,* & *Happy LGBTQ Wrath Month*), and has written for Look Up Records (Seattle), and *Deep Overstock*: The Bookseller's Journal. He also founded the podcast & small press publishing house, The Poet Heroic, and founded the digital magic space The Healers Coven. He also showcases his psychedelic makeup skills as the phenomenal drag queen Tabitha Acidz.
Find more at: www.timothyarlissobrien.com

Kathryn Paulsen
Kathryn Paulsen writes poetry, prose, plays, and screenplays. Her work has appeared in publications from Canada to Ireland to Australia, including *The New York Times, The Stinging Fly, Humber Literary Review, Scum, Spillway, Craft, Isthmus, Big Fiction*, and the *London Reader*, and she's received residence grants at Yaddo, MacDowell, and other retreats. She lives in New York City but, having grown up in a military family, has roots in many places. The summer after her freshman year in college, she worked as an assistant to the librarian of the Altus (Oklahoma) Air Force Base Library, where she first made the acquaintance of James Bond, thanks to a recommendation by one of the patrons.

Diana Raab, PhD
Diana Raab, PhD, is an award-winning memoirist, poet, blogger, speaker, and author of 13 books. Her new poetry chapbook is, *An Imaginary Affair: Poems Whispered to Neruda* (Finishing Line Press, 2022). She blogs for Psychology Today, Thrive Global, Sixty and Me, Good Men Project, and The Wisdom Daily. Visit: www.dianaraab.com.

Justin Ratcliff
Justin Ratcliff is a new emerging poet, who was cast into the depths of himself during the Covid-19 outbreak. Born, raised, and still preceding in South Central Alaska. From a very early age he had found a haven in his local library. Each new book was a new world in which to escape the harsh realities of life's bitter brew. Draws much of his inspirations from psychology, philosophy, theology, nature, and dark fantasy.

Joy Richu
Introducing Joy Richu, an accomplished illustrator whose artistry thrives on the power of storytelling. With a unique background in Design and Creative Writing, Joy's work celebrates the profound beauty of the human experience,

whether it's in our remarkable discoveries, boundless imagination, or the creation of meaningful, inclusive communities. Her portfolio boasts collaborations with prestigious clients like The New York Times, Mastercard Foundation, Diageo, Lancet, and more. A true chameleon, Joy seamlessly adapts her artistic style to meet the specific needs of each client while maintaining her own signature touch. Passionate about fostering connections, Joy invites you to engage further by following her Instagram @joyrichu or exploring her website at www.joyrichu.com.

Michael Santiago

Michael Santiago is a serial expat, avid traveler, and writer of all kinds. Originally from New York City, and later relocating to Rome in 2016 and Nanjing in 2018. He enjoys the finer things in life like walks on the beach, existential conversations and swapping murder mystery ideas. Keen on exploring themes of humanity within a fictitious context and aspiring author.

George Sarnat

Gerard Sarnat has been nominated for the pending Science Fiction Poetry Association Dwarf Star Award, won San Francisco Poetry's 2020 Contest, the Poetry in the Arts First Place Award plus the Dorfman Prize, and has been nominated for handfuls of Pushcarts plus Best of the Net Awards. Gerry is widely published including in 2023 San Diego Poetry Annual, 2022 Awakenings Review, 2022 Arts & Cultural Council of Bucks County Celebration, 2022 Rio Grande Valley International Poetry Festival Anthology, Pocket Samovar, Free State, The Broken City, Sandy River Review, Three Rooms Press/Maintenant, New World Writing, The Font, BigCityLit, HitchLit Review, Lowestoft, Washington Square Review, University of British Columbia and University of Chicago and University of Virginia presses. He is a Harvard College and Medical School-trained physician who's built and staffed clinics for the disenfranchised as well as a Stanford professor and healthcare CEO. Currently he is devoting energy/resources to deal with climate justice, and serves on Climate Action Now's board. Gerry's been married since 1969 with progeny consisting of four collections (Homeless Chronicles: From Abraham To Burning Man, Disputes, 17s, Melting the Ice King).

Junix Seraphim

At 17, Junix Seraphim started their first over-the-table work as a bookseller at Barnes & Noble in the mall. When that wasn't enough to pay their rent, bills, and put themselves through community college, they moved to Powell's where they also worked as a bookseller. Today, Junix is a poet, drag king, and grassroots organizer fighting for the rights and livelihoods of

Filipinos in the homeland and in the belly of the beast, the U.S. Their love of goth culture and black lipstick is reflected in his drag performances, which range from campy character drag to macabre explorations of his personal relationship with death, and the relationships with death held by their communities. Junix and their friends are actively shaping the transsexual future.

Jihye Shin
Jihye Shin is a Korean-American poet and bookseller based in Florida.

Francesca J. Sidoti
In college I worked at the campus bookstore as well at a stationery store specializing in writing supplies. At the time, the college bookstore was a Barnes & Noble. This was long in the past, but I have maintained an affinity for bookstores, particularly independent bookshops. Every time we go on vacation or a weekend getaway, we seek out the local, interesting offbeat bookstore for an afternoon browse.
My work has been published in *Chiron Review, Haight-Ashbury LIterary Journal, South Ash Press, Viet Nam Generation, Connections* and other literary magazines; however, this is my first submission in 25 years. I have just recently returned to submitting my work for publication following a 25-year hiatus. As a featured reader I have appeared in bookstores and other venues throughout the US and Canada. I am grateful over the years to have received several awards, most recently the Dorn Space 2021 Poet of the Year.

Ranjith Sivaraman
Ranjith Sivaraman is an upcoming Poet from Kerala, a beautiful state in India. His poems merge nature imagery, human emotions, and human psychology into a gorgeous tapestry. Sivaraman's English Poems are published in International Literature Magazines and Journals from various locations like Alberta, Budapest, Essex, London, New York, Indiana, Lisbon, Colorado, California, New Jersey, Tk'emlúps te Secwepemc, Kerala, Texas, Chennai & Toronto. His poem 'Shortest Distance' was released as Music Video in 2022. insta Handle: @lovelifetip Please visit ranjithsivaraman.com/selected-work/ for more of his works.

Karen Sleeth
Karen Sleeth receives an MFA in Creative Writing from Lindenwood University in May 2023. Her work has appeared or is forthcoming in *The Main Street Rag, 2022 Best of Potato Soup Journal, Hard to Find: An Anthology of New Southern Gothic, Lost and Found – 2023 Personal Story Publishing Project*, and others.

Rin Stone
My name is Rin Stone, and I'm a trans guy from Alabama living in Portland, Oregon. I work at Powell's City of Books where I specialize in Autistic and queer books. Most of my writings are songs, poetry, or journal entries about experiencing the world as a queer Autistic person.

K. B. Thomas
K. B. Thomas has been a book lover and bookseller since dinosaurs roamed the earth. She works, writes, and walks her dog in Portland, OR. Find more fiction at: kbthomas.net

Nam Hoang Tran
Nam Hoang Tran is a writer and visual artist based in Orlando, FL. His work appears or is forthcoming in *Posit, Bending Genres, Midway Journal, BlazeVOX, New Delta Review, Diode*, and elsewhere. Find him online at www.namhtran.com.

Renee Williams
Renee Williams is a retired English professor, who has written for *Of Rust and Glass*, Alien Buddha Press and the *New Verse News*.

Z.B. Wagman
Z.B. Wagman is an editor for the *Deep Overstock Literary Journal* and a co-host of the Deep Overstock Fiction podcast. When not writing or editing he can be found behind the desk at the Beaverton City Library, where he finds much inspiration.

Alixa Writes
A law student by day, Alixa writes poetry by night.

Nicholas Yandell
Nicholas Yandell is a composer, who sometimes creates with words instead of sound. In those cases, he usually ends up with fiction and occasionally poetry. He also paints and draws, and often all these activities become combined, because they're really not all that different from each other, and it's all just art right?
When not working on creative projects, Nick works as a bookseller at Powell's Books in Portland, Oregon, where he enjoys being surrounded by a wealth of knowledge, as well as working and interacting with creatively stimulating people. He has a website where he displays his creations; it's nicholasyandell.com. Check it out!

www.ingramcontent.com/pod-product-compliance
Lightning Source LLC
Chambersburg PA
CBHW061456210726
48287CB00007B/2528